JENNA ST. JAMES

COPYRIGHT © 2017 BY JENNA ST. JAMES.
PUBLISHED BY JENNA ST. JAMES
COVER DESIGN BY JULIANA BUHMAN

Cheryl,
Enjoy!
Jenna!

JENNA ST. JAMES BOOKS

Ryli Sinclair Mystery Series Order

Picture Perfect Murder
Girls' Night Out Murder
Old-Fashioned Murder
Bed, Breakfast, and Murder
Veiled in Murder
Bachelorettes and Bodies
Rings, Veils, and Murder
Last Stop Murder

Sullivan Sisters Mystery Series Order

Murder on the Vine
Burning Hot Murder
Prepear to Die

DEDICATION

To Gretchen Allen…thank you for keeping me motivated and talking me off ledges I'd love to leap from. And for also just talking with me about silly things. I believe the longest e-mail chain I counted was fourteen responses in a matter of hours. You have a way of making me feel like you have all the time in the world to answer my questions. LOL…I know better! So thank you!

Amy Johnson…thank you for the countless hours you've spent chatting with me and encouraging me. Your positive outlook has been such a help to me. Blessings to you and your family!

To Jane Dietz…thanks for helping me with hotel security questions. If I flubbed anything up, just glance right over. LOL.

To my Grams, Beulah Mills, who inspires me to be Aunt Shirley…mainly because my Grams is both horrified and honored to be my Aunt Shirley inspiration. When I called her on the phone to ask her how she plays craps (and she does play it well), it took only thirty minutes to learn all her trade secrets! Too bad I don't play!

And, as always, to my mom and sister. I love you more than peanut butter!

CHAPTER 1

"Vegas, baby!" My great-Aunt Shirley stuck her pink and purple head out of Mom's Tahoe and bellowed a war whoop before plopping back down in her seat. "Oh, yeah. Cruisin' the Strip. I could get used to this."

My about-to-pop best friend, Paige, giggled as she gently rubbed a hand over her protruding belly.

"You holding up okay?" I asked.

"Yep," Paige nodded.

I'd worried like crazy Paige wouldn't be able to come on my bachelorette trip—a five-day stay in Las Vegas. Originally Paige's due date was mid-November, but now that she's been diagnosed—and yes, I did just say diagnosed—with twins, she's been told she could safely deliver at thirty-six weeks. Since Paige was at week thirty-four right now, we weren't sure if she should chance it.

Of course, the Vegas bachelorette thing was *not* my idea...it was Aunt Shirley's. Again, no surprise there. It also wouldn't be a surprise if Aunt Shirley decided to stay and become a Vegas showgirl, either. If they even did that sort of thing anymore.

"Don't get me wrong," Aunt Shirley continued as she mock-glared at Paige, "it's no Falcon road trip, but it'll do."

The Falcon Aunt Shirley referred to was her pride and joy—and now my pride and joy—1965 turquoise Ford Falcon with purple flames on the sides. It had a stock 302 with an Edelbrock fuel injection. The barely-there dashboard was done in the same turquoise color, and the bucket seats in the front and bench seat in the back were pristine white with turquoise stitching.

Unfortunately, this far along in her pregnancy, Paige couldn't fly. So driving was our only option. She and mom put their foot down and said no way would Paige be riding in the Falcon eighteen hours. Paige was to be pampered the whole time.

Even though I was a little disappointed, I couldn't fault them. The Falcon didn't have modern amenities like heated seats and plush cushions, so it was a no-brainer to take Mom's Tahoe.

It was still a tight squeeze with five of us—Mom, Mindy, Paige, Aunt Shirley, and me—and our suitcases. So much so, Mom and I went together and packed one suitcase between us.

"Has anyone spoken to the boys?" Mom asked from the driver's seat.

"I haven't spoken to Garrett since we left Colorado this morning," I said.

We'd stopped overnight in Colorado since it was a half-way point.

"I texted Matt a couple hours ago and he said everything was quiet at the station," Paige said.

My soon-to-be husband and former military hottie, Garrett Kimble, was the police chief for the Granville Police Department. And in a few short weeks, I would no longer be Ryli Jo Sinclair...but Ryli Jo Kimble.

"No talking about men on this trip," Aunt Shirley snapped. "Good for nothing beasts!"

I chuckled at Aunt Shirley's sudden discomfort. Ever since Old Man Jenkins came to her rescue a couple months ago, she's been having a hard time escaping him. He'd once told her the next time she needed his help, that his payment would be marriage. And don't you know Aunt Shirley ended up needing his help...and she's been dodging him ever since.

I loved Old Man Jenkins. He was an eighty-five-year-old former military man who loved to wear Speedos when he swam and thought Aunt Shirley hung the moon and stars. Personally, I thought she was an idiot for turning down his marriage proposals.

5

Not a lot of people could handle—or would even want to *try* and handle—my Aunt Shirley.

Aunt Shirley was a true old maid. She'd never married nor had kids. Instead, she ran away to Los Angeles when she was in her early twenties and became a private investigator. I think she's around seventy-five, but I'm not sure. Now she and I work as reporters at the *Granville Gazette,* the town paper that Mindy and her husband, Hank, own.

"I see the hotel," Mindy squealed from the front seat, her platinum blonde hair bouncing up and down. She always wore skin-tight Capri pants, neon colored off-the-shoulder shirts, and designer high-heeled shoes. "And it's incredible!"

I peered down and tried to see out the window. Between the suitcases and Aunt Shirley's multi-colored head, I couldn't see much. I glanced out Paige's window and marveled at the magnificent buildings and the sights, sounds, and smells coming through the windows.

Mom veered right and we pulled in under a huge semi-circle valet-parking area that led to the entrance of the hotel. I know it may seem like a crazy thing to do, but I let Aunt Shirley plan my bachelorette party. Usually it's the Maid of Honor's duty, but Paige was in no condition...and I'm not gonna lie, I knew Aunt Shirley would do a much better job.

Everything about the next five days was going to be a complete surprise for me. And I couldn't be happier. I had the four most important women in my life with me, and we were ready to have a good time. And by good time, I hope I mean spa treatments, fabulous dinners, and a few drinks thrown in. But with Aunt Shirley at the helm, you never knew.

We piled out of the Tahoe as Mom talked with the valet attendant. I opened the back and helped another valet pile our luggage onto a rolling cart. Outside of the vehicle, the sounds were almost deafening. I'd never been to Vegas before...or really any casino for that matter. While Kansas City does have boats you can gamble on, it's just something I'd never done.

Paige grasped my hand and together we looked up at the roof of the hotel. Or at least I tried to. I got dizzy and looked down quickly. Once the bags were loaded, we strolled into the hotel and casino.

If I thought the sounds outside were loud, I was sadly mistaken. Between the bells, whistles, screams, and sirens going off on myriad machines, I could hardly hear myself think. We found the elevator and pushed the number that would take us to the mezzanine to check in.

"I went with a French-inspired hotel, Ryli," Aunt Shirley said with a twinkle in her eye. "Everything from our suite, to the five-star restaurant, to the entertainment for your bachelorette party will revolve in some way around a French inspiration."

The elevator opened onto the mezzanine and my first real glimpse of the hotel took my breath away.

"It's perfect already," I said honestly.

And it was.

Gleaming white tile floor as far as the eye could see, Cathedral ceilings covered in golds and whites, countless chandeliers so big if one fell it'd take out at least four bodies.

Morbid but true.

"You think this is perfect," Aunt Shirley boasted, "wait until you see the room."

For the first time since we started on the trip, I got a little niggling in the back of my mind. How much was this trip costing exactly? I mean, I pitched in for gas—over Mom's major objections—but this hotel had to cost a bundle.

Half an hour later as I pushed open the hotel room, I knew my suspicions were correct. A few months back I'd met a woman named Virginia who had the most amazing furniture. Since then, I've started scouring the Internet for finds on certain pieces. I knew expensive furniture.

"I have your bags," the porter said from inside the suite.

I slowly made my way farther into the room, trying to take in everything at once. There were two settees done in cream and light blues and one chair that looked like a Louis XV inspiration.

"I have been informed," the porter said as he gently took me by the arm and ushered me into the master bedroom, "that as the guest of honor, you get the master suite."

A large, four-poster bed with a white ruffled comforter and sky blue pillows was pushed against a wall. Two armoires were also pushed against opposite walls, and a small door led to the bathroom. I was almost scared to see what the luxurious bathroom looked like.

"Enjoy your stay, Mademoiselle."

I walked over to a window and ran my hand over the plush drapery that billowed out and fell in a puddle at the floor. The cream-colored fabric felt soft to the touch.

"This room is for you and Paige," Aunt Shirley said from the doorway. "There are two other small rooms that we are staying in. Your mom and Mindy in one, and I'll take the other."

"Who's paying for this?" I asked. "I know this has to cost a pretty penny. And the fact we're staying here four nights…well, I'd hate to even add that up in my head."

"Come sit," Aunt Shirley said as she shuffled over to the bed, sat down, then patted a spot next to her on the bed.

I ambled over to where she was and sat down, never once taking my eyes off of her.

"You know I never had children. Heck, I've never even been married. That being said, I do have a substantial savings from all the years I worked as a private investigator." Aunt Shirley leaned in closer. "Plus, I once had a famous Hollywood movie star—and I'm not going to say who—give me some financial advice that worked out pretty well in my favor."

I couldn't help but smile. Nothing Aunt Shirley loved more than to flaunt all the Hollywood men she used to date back in the day.

"This has to cost—"

"You're not understanding what I'm saying to you." I flinched at the sharpness in Aunt Shirley's voice. Something I rarely heard from her. "This is my gift to you, Ryli. My personal gift. This is my way of thanking you for keeping me around, taking me places, including me in your life."

Tears sprang to my eyes, and I tried to blink them back. I didn't want to cry on my first night. Maybe the second, but definitely not the first.

Aunt Shirley reached over and grabbed my face in her wrinkled hands. "Let me do this for you." A wicked grin slowly spread over her face. "Besides, you haven't seen anything yet. There will be lots of little things along the way, but wait until you see what I did for your bachelorette party. You'll be thanking me for years to come."

I groaned. That sounded dangerous and ominous. And I suddenly couldn't help but grin back at her.

"Thank you, Aunt Shirley. I know I don't say it often, but you really have been inspirational in helping me grow up this past year."

Aunt Shirley patted me on my knee and stood up. "That's my job. Now, I'll leave you alone. I'm sure you want to give that man of yours a call."

As she closed the door, I pulled out my cell and called Garrett.

"Kimble here."

"Sinclair here. Soon-to-be Kimble," I joked.

"Sin! I'm glad you called. Are you in Vegas yet?"

I looked around the posh, French-styled room and laughed. "Vegas or France. I'm not sure."

I filled him in on the fabulous hotel and French-themed trip Aunt Shirley had planned for us. "Everything from the room, to the food, to our entertainment."

Garrett growled. "Those French can be quite risqué. Don't make me fly over there and bail you out of jail."

I laughed. "Don't worry. I promise not to do anything that lands me in jail or gets me into trouble."

Sometimes I just don't know when to keep my mouth shut.

CHAPTER 2

"I'm not even sure I have the words to describe how amazing this hotel is," Paige said as she struggled into her Arabian blue maternity dress. "Aunt Shirley definitely did right by you."

I stepped out of the ensuite bathroom and tried not to look guilty. "I know. I still feel badly she's spending all this money on me. I mean, we even get our own bathroom while those three are sharing one."

Paige finally stopped struggling into her dress and mock-glared at me. "Ryli Jo, you know they don't mind. They're doing this for you. They want this to be the best trip ever. You'll only get to do a bachelorette party once."

"Thank goodness. Remember yours?"

Paige's bachelorette party had two dead bodies, a half-naked Aunt Shirley bribing a police officer to strip for a buck, and ultimately Aunt Shirley and I held at gunpoint by a killer.

"We are definitely *not* going to have a repeat performance of my bachelorette party," Paige said. "No one should ever have to go through that."

"How do I look?" I smoothed down the maroon halter dress that stopped just short of my knees.

Paige scowled. "I hate you for being able to wear that." Tears suddenly filled her eyes. "I can't even get my shoes on."

I hid my smile as I coaxed her onto the bed and helped her slip on her shoes before I stepped into my own gold and silver sandals.

"Let's go find out if this restaurant Aunt Shirley picked out is any good," I joked as I hauled her up on her feet.

"I'm so hungry I could eat a horse," Paige groaned.

I wrinkled my nose. "This is supposed to be a five-star French restaurant. I don't think horse is on the menu."

Paige laughed and slid her arms through mine. "Thanks for making me laugh. Just don't do it too much...my bladder isn't what it used to be."

***

"Aunt Shirley, your restaurant pick is right on," Mindy said as she took a sip of her Aperol spritzer. "The food looks and smells amazing, and the drinks are strong and yummy."

The restaurant was running a few minutes behind, so they sent us to the bar to relax and have a drink while we waited. Poor Paige was a little miffed she couldn't participate in the festivities. I tried not to enjoy her pouting too much.

"Whaddaya think so far?" Aunt Shirley asked.

I turned to her and smiled. Even though the restaurant was posh, I didn't have to worry about Aunt Shirley going all sophisticated and glamorous on me. Her yellow, purple, and teal skirt, pared with bright purple top, and purple and pink hair screamed, "Look at me. I love being the center of attention." And it looked great on her.

"I think if the food is anywhere near as good as these drinks, I'm going to kiss your feet and call you queen."

Aunt Shirley threw back her head and laughed. "Get ready to pucker up, little girl."

"Do you need to sit down?" Mom asked Paige.

Paige, looking like she was ready to fall over on her feet, shook her head and rubbed her stomach. "These little devils are fighting and jockeying for position tonight. I'm not sure what hurts more...my ribs, kidneys, stomach, back."

I bit my lip and frowned. "Gosh, you make it sound so appealing. I can't wait for Garrett and me to start a family of our own."

Paige laughed. "I'm sorry, Ryli. It really is amazing. I'm just feeling a little sorry for myself. You'll love being pregnant."

I wasn't convinced.

One of the drawbacks of marrying someone ten years older than you...they're gonna want to start a family soon. I knew that going into the deal, but my mind was still balking. I could barely remember to feed myself and my cat...thinking about another adult and baby thrown into the picture was starting to give me hives.

"That's us," Mindy said as she held up a blinking pager.

The maître d led us to a large, round table near the back of the restaurant. I was excited to see we were near the kitchen. This would give me an opportunity to see all the delicious food coming out. I may not be able to cook very well, but I had a healthy appreciation for food.

"Might I suggest tonight the ratatouille with a glass of Cotes du Rhone or the steak au poivre with a glass of Chateauneuf-du-Pape. Both are exquisite choices."

The maître d looked at us expectantly. And I'm not ashamed to say I had no idea what the man was saying. Luckily I was saved from having to reply when a commotion from the kitchen caught my attention. I leaned back in my chair and caught a glimpse of an imposing man in a tall white hat and white coat arguing with a gentleman in a black suit.

"Excusez moi," the maître d said as he scooted backward a few steps before pivoting and heading for the kitchen.

I picked up the sheet of paper and looked over the choices. After a few frustrating minutes, I put the paper down and looked around at other people's food. This was obviously the way I was going to have to order, because I had no idea about anything on the paper.

The kitchen door opened and a server carried out three dishes. One of them caught my eye, and I watched what table it went to. That was gonna be my dinner.

Another server came out of the kitchen and in my peripheral I saw the two men still exchanging angry words. Not for the first time I wished I had bionic hearing. Nothing I loved more than a juicy story.

Our server came by to take our orders. Everyone was able to order off the paper except me. I pointed to the table that had the dinner I wanted. I accepted the chuckles around the table…along with another glass of wine.

"What's on the agenda tonight after dinner?" I asked.

Paige groaned. "I hope you don't take this the wrong way, but I'm probably going to go back up to the room and rest."

"Me, too," Mom said. "I'm pretty tired from all the driving I've done the last two days. Once I have a good night's sleep, I'll be raring to go. I promise."

A little disappointed, I tried not to take it personally. I understood why they were tired. I'd just hoped for a fun first night.

"I'm ready to hit the slots after this," Aunt Shirley exclaimed.

I smiled and took another drink of my fabulous wine. At least I could count on Aunt Shirley to keep the party going.

Our meal arrived and I dug in with gusto. Turned out I'd ordered the special, steak au poivre, and just like the maître d promised…it did not disappoint.

"Good evening. Is everything to your satisfaction?"

I was surprised to see the gentleman from the kitchen in the black suit standing next to me. He didn't look like he'd just gone a few rounds with the imposing chef. In fact, he looked pretty delicious with his slicked back brown hair, mocha colored eyes, and flirtatious smile. He was also a lot younger than I originally thought. Maybe forty.

"My name is Philippe Bernard, and I'm the manager. If you need anything, please let me or the assistant manager, Holly Barrows, know."

He pointed to a woman on the other side of the large restaurant. She was dressed in a black skirt that came to her knees, high heels, and a long-sleeved blazer over an undershirt. Just looking at her made me want to break out in a sweat. Her blonde hair was pulled back in a bun so severe her eyebrows were practically stretched to her temple. Large, red-framed glasses covered half of her face. I pegged her for thirtyish, even though she was dressed far older than she really was.

"Thank you, Philippe," Aunt Shirley said with a wink. "We'll keep you in mind if we need you for anything." She wiggled her brows at him lewdly.

Philippe threw back his head and laughed. "You do that. Bon appétit."

The meals were all delicious, and we each took turns tasting the many dishes splayed out around the table. By the time the after-dinner digestive drink of Cognac was served—a *fabulous* French tradition as far as I was concerned—my belly was stuffed and I was feeling a little tipsy.

I grabbed my purse and practically waddled out into the lobby of the casino. The bright lights and whistles had me itching to play. There was an excitement in the air that called to me.

"You're sure you don't mind us going back to the room?" Mindy asked.

I gave them all a hug. "Not in the least. Aunt Shirley and I will be fine."

Mom looked leery. "I know I should believe that…but I'm a little hesitant."

I laughed and pushed her toward the elevator.

"Don't wait up!" Aunt Shirley called out to them gleefully as they disappeared from sight.

"Thanks for the wonderful dinner." I slid my arm through Aunt Shirley's and we ambled off to find us a slot machine to throw away some money.

An hour later, I was down nearly thirty dollars but having a great time with Aunt Shirley. The floor girl coming by every twenty minutes or so to give us watered down drinks helped ease the pain of losing.

"That good for nothing swindler!"

I looked over to the older woman sitting at my right and then followed her gaze. She was watching an elderly couple walk across the casino floor laughing and having a good time.

"Excuse me?" I asked.

The lady sniffed back tears as she dug into her purse for a tissue. "That man is a swindler. He hustled me out of both money and jewelry."

"Say what!" Aunt Shirley exclaimed on my left. She popped up out of her seat and stood behind my chair. "What happened?"

The woman blew out a breath and took a long drink from her glass. She was a strikingly attractive woman around seventy. Her silver hair was styled in a classic bob that was feathered back on each side, and her jewelry looked to be real and expensive. She ran a hand down her gray tunic before answering. "My name is Cheryl Owens, and I'm here on the Senior Getaway Trip. Once a year a group of seniors come to the casino for a week to meet and have fun. Most of us are from Nevada, but there are some who have traveled from California and Arizona. This is my third time attending."

"It sounds like fun," I offered gently when she dabbed at her eyes.

"It is. Only this year, we have a guy in our group from California that's swindling all the elderly ladies. I think I was his second. And by the looks of it, Eleanor will be his third."

"Do you know Eleanor?" Aunt Shirley asked. "Can you tell her what's going on?"

Cheryl Owens shrugged. "I met her last year, but I don't really know her."

"What did he do to you?" I asked.

A Burning Hot Murder

Cheryl took a deep breath. "I lost my husband five years ago, and it took me a long time to get over him. But three years ago, I decided I needed to get on with my life. So I signed up for this trip, and it's been a life-changing experience every year. Two nights ago, I met Arthur Tisdale and things have went downhill since. Arthur took me out to dinner, then conveniently forgot his wallet. I paid for dinner and said yes to dancing." Cheryl's lips pursed and her eyes narrowed. "I guess some of it's my fault because I had a couple drinks and was having a great time. When we went back up to my room, he asked to come in for a nightcap. I know I should have said no, but I let him in. When he went to take a drink, he slipped and his drink went all down the front of him." She paused and wiped a tear. "It was so stupid of me. I told him to hold tight...I'd run and get a towel to clean him up. While I was getting a towel wet, he was in my room pilfering my jewelry."

I gasped in surprise. I thought back to the little old man I saw laughing and walking across the casino and had a hard time picturing him as a thief.

"I didn't notice until later that night when I went to take off the jewelry I was wearing." Tears streamed down Cheryl's contorted face. "He stole a ring my husband had given me on our fortieth wedding anniversary."

"That snake!" Aunt Shirley exclaimed. "Did you tell anyone?"

Cheryl nodded. "I mentioned it at breakfast the next morning, and Mildred Biggins admitted the same thing had happened to her!"

"Have you told the hotel security?" I asked. "Surely they can do something."

Cheryl shook her head. "I suppose I should, but I'm just so humiliated. I can't believe I fell for his lines. And then to bring him into my room." She closed her eyes for a few seconds. "I'm afraid people will get the wrong idea. But now I'm afraid Eleanor is going to get swindled like Mildred Biggins and I did."

Aunt Shirley rested her hands on Cheryl's shoulders. "Don't you worry. My niece and I will take care of this for you."

I whipped my head around to stare incredulously at Aunt Shirley. Was she insane? How on earth were we going to fix this for these women?

"This is right up our alley," Aunt Shirley went on, ignoring my stare. "We've help solve over five crimes this year alone. We can help you."

I bit back a groan. While I understood where Aunt Shirley was coming from…this was still my bachelorette trip. I didn't want to spend it chasing after an old guy scamming women.

I looked over at Cheryl and read the hope in her eyes. There was no way Aunt Shirley would back down now. With her, it was in for a penny, in for a pound.

I sighed. "Tell us everything about this Arthur Tisdale, and we'll come up with a plan."

CHAPTER 3

"Thanks for offering to help with this," Aunt Shirley said as we strolled to the elevator an hour later. It was almost ten o'clock, and I was dead tired.

After a lot of deliberation, Cheryl, Aunt Shirley, and I came up with a tentative plan to get Cheryl's jewelry back and to teach Arthur Tisdale a lesson. Cheryl said she'd talk with Mildred, and the two of them would meet up with us tomorrow morning to finalize how to con the con man.

Our shoes clicked rhythmically against the tile as we walked out of the casino floor and into the enormous entertainment and food service area. There were two performance theaters directly across from each other, along with four or five restaurants lining the white gleaming lobby.

"Hey, look," Aunt Shirley said, pointing to the French restaurant we'd eaten at earlier. "It's the fuzz. There must be four cops standing by the door."

"I think you're seeing double from all the drinks you had tonight," I giggle. But like a moth to a flame, we both scurried over to the restaurant. Aunt Shirley was right. I counted two cops manning the door, and two more inside talking with patrons.

"What's going on?" Aunt Shirley asked one of the cops.

"You need to step back, ma'am. This is a police matter."

"We were just eating here a little bit ago," Aunt Shirley continued as though she hadn't heard the officer.

He narrowed his eyes at us. "How long ago?"

Aunt Shirley shrugged. "Can't be too sure. I didn't look at my watch."

Nice and vague. Keep him guessing. Good job, Aunt Shirley!

The young officer sighed and motioned us in. I tried my best to squelch my excitement. Especially since I wasn't sure if it was from too many free drinks at the slots or what. But my Spidey senses were definitely tingling.

"Wait right here," the police officer said, "and I'll let the detective in charge know you may have seen something."

I tried hard not to ogle the young officer's butt as he walked away. I really missed Garrett.

"Did we see something?" Aunt Shirley asked.

I bit my lip and rocked my hand from side to side. "Maybe."

Aunt Shirley's eyes sharpened. "Like what?"

I watched as the young officer took an older gentleman aside and spoke with him. I inched my way closer to where the kitchen staff was huddled together. Aunt Shirley followed without making a sound.

When I felt we were close enough to not get in trouble but yet still hear what was going on, I turned back to Aunt Shirley. "Tonight when we were being seated, I heard a commotion in the kitchen. When the door swung open, that guy right there," I surreptitiously pointed to the guy in the tall, white hat and white coat, "was yelling at the manager, Philippe." I looked around the room but didn't see Philippe.

"Why didn't you tell me?" Aunt Shirley demanded. Odd since her gaze hadn't strayed from where the detective and police officer were talking.

I shrugged. "I didn't think it was important."

Aunt Shirley didn't say anything. If ever there was a time to yell at me, it was then. Saying I didn't think something was important was like throwing gasoline on a fire. To Aunt Shirley, everything was important when it came to solving a case.

When she didn't react, I snapped my fingers in front of her face. "Earth to Aunt Shirley. What's going on? Why aren't you paying attention?"

"I am."

20

I put my hand under her chin and turned her gaze to mine. "Now you're looking at me. What's got you so enthralled?"

Aunt Shirley narrowed her eyes. "I don't know. Something about that detective is familiar."

I scoffed. "Maybe he's been on one of those reality cop shows you watch."

Aunt Shirley scowled at me, and I couldn't help but snicker. "Well, how else would you know someone here in Vegas?"

"Not sure."

The young officer pointed in our direction and I saw the detective's brow furrow. He nodded to the officer and wearily turned and went back to work asking a middle-aged couple questions.

"I just don't understand why this happened," a female voice to my right said.

"I'm surprised it didn't happen weeks ago," a male countered. "Chef hasn't been himself for a month now."

I turned to the two voices so I could hear more.

"I know," the young girl said shyly. "I just can't believe it finally happened."

What finally happened?

"Do you think they'll arrest him?" the young girl asked the man.

The skinny, dark-haired man barked out a laugh. "Yeah. I mean, half the kitchen staff saw them arguing tonight."

The young girl bit her lip and looked back at the man in the tall hat and white coat.

"Hi," I said. "My name is Ryli and this is Aunt Shirley. I couldn't help but overhear. What's going on?"

The man slid his gaze over me but said nothing.

Luckily the girl was more forthcoming.

"Our manager, Philippe Bernard, was murdered tonight."

My mouth dropped open. "Oh no! I remember him stopping by our table tonight."

A Burning Hot Murder

I wondered why Aunt Shirley hadn't jumped in yet with her exclamation. I looked over and saw her still staring at the lead detective.

The skinny, dark-haired man narrowed his eyes at me. "I thought I recognized you. Didn't I wait on you tonight? Like hours ago? Why are you here?"

"We saw something," Aunt Shirley finally said. "A fight in the kitchen that involved your manager."

Good guess.

The young girl hunched her shoulders and twisted her hands together. "You saw Chef and Mr. Bernard arguing? I was afraid others would hear."

Our server from tonight narrowed his gaze at Aunt Shirley. "How? Your back was to the kitchen."

"Mine wasn't," I answered somewhat smartly.

"My name is Daisy," the girl said as she stuck her hand out to me. "This is Rod."

I reached over and shook her hand. He didn't offer his.

"Like I said, my name is Ryli and this is Aunt Shirley."

Rod leaned in and whispered something to Daisy. Whatever it was caused her to flinch and nod. He strode away without another glance at us.

"Rod's just sensitive," Daisy said by way of apology.

Yeah, he's all heart.

"What do you think happened tonight?" Aunt Shirley asked.

Daisy bit her lip and gazed over to where Rod had departed. He was leaning against a wall, arms crossed over his chest, scowling at us.

Daisy shrugged and didn't make eye contact. "I don't know."

I leaned in. "Look, Daisy, my aunt and I—"

I broke off. How many times had I told Aunt Shirley not to tell people we seem to stumble into murder and dead bodies as easily as some people breathe.

"What my niece is trying to say," Aunt Shirley jumped in, "is that this is sort of what we do. We've solved about five or six murders this year alone."

I winced. It sounded bad when she said it like that. Like dead bodies just fall at our feet at every turn.

Don't they?

Daisy's eyes widened. "Really? Here in Las Vegas?"

I shook my head. "No. We're from Missouri. My family and I are here for my bachelorette party."

"Congratulations!" Her smile faltered. "I'm sorry you got involved with this."

For some weird reason, I really wasn't sorry. Usually when Aunt Shirley and I stumbled across a dead body, she had to pull me in kicking and screaming to solve the case. I sucked in my breath at the thought that maybe I was getting used to it. Or worse…maybe I was enjoying it. Enjoying the thrill of solving a murder.

Stop it! It's just the alcohol talking!

"Have you spoken to the detective in charge yet?" Aunt Shirley asked.

Daisy nodded.

"Can you tell us what you told him?" Aunt Shirley asked. "Maybe what he asked you?"

"Sure. I don't see why not. You guys are practically detectives yourself."

Neither Aunt Shirley nor I corrected her.

"Okay. So sometime tonight our manager, Philippe Bernard, was murdered."

CHAPTER 4

"How do you know he was murdered as opposed to just died from natural causes?" Aunt Shirley asked.

Tears welled up in Daisy's eyes. "Because he had duct tape over his mouth, and his hands were duct taped to the arms of his chair, and—"

Daisy sobbed into her tissue. I turned to block her. No sense in bringing undo attention to her.

And then to us.

"And?" Aunt Shirley prompted.

"And his femoral artery was cut."

Whoa! That's some serious anger right there.

"So he had duct tape over his mouth and hands, and his femoral artery was cut?" Aunt Shirley clarified.

The girl nodded before looking up at me. "Poor Maureen. I'll never forget her scream. Or the look on her face when she ran out of the office."

"Who's Maureen?" I asked.

Daisy looked up through her lashes, trying not to turn her head. "See the woman sitting in the chair over there. That's Maureen. She's the head server. She's pretty much in charge of the floor."

Turning casually to look at someone is never easy. At least not for me. But I tried it anyway. I took in the woman's appearance. Shoulder-length copper brown hair with a natural wave. Gaunt, drawn in features. Although I was pretty sure her drastically pale complexion was due to the shock more than her lack of sunlight. Beneath the surface, I could tell she had a cute, pixie-like face and a strong, athletic body. If I had to guess, I'd say she was in her late thirties.

"Were Maureen and Philippe Bernard dating?" I asked.

"Oh, no." Daisy looked around as though checking to make sure no one else overheard. She leaned in and whispered, "At least, I don't think so. She and Chef Benoit have been kinda seeing each other for a while now. Though none of us are supposed to know. Maureen and Chef Benoit in a relationship would be frowned upon."

"And this Chef Benoit is a big deal?" I asked.

Daisy nodded her head vigorously. "Chef Benoit has been the head chef here for about seven years now."

"And why can't Maureen and Chef Benoit be in a relationship?" Aunt Shirley asked.

"Because they hold top, key positions in the restaurant. It's just not done. Management would definitely frown on coworkers dating." Daisy's cheeks turned pink. "Plus, usually chefs of Chef Benoit's station don't date 'the help' if you will. I mean, he's a pretty famous chef around Vegas."

I looked over at the man who was obviously the head chef—the man in the tall, white hat and white coat. He was just under six-foot tall and broad in the shoulders. Even hidden under a white coat I could tell his arms were muscular and thick. His face was weathered and chiseled in that distinguished look men tend to develop as they get older. I couldn't tell his hair color due to the hat, but I could see whiffs of gray in his sideburns.

"Handsome," I mused.

Daisy grinned at me. "Chef? Yeah, he is." Daisy looked over at Chef Benoit, her grin faltering. "But lately, we've all noticed that Mr. Bernard was paying a lot more attention to Maureen than he should."

You don't say.

Daisy rubbed a hand vigorously up and down her arm. "Even though the fight in the kitchen tonight was about food preparation and the menu specials, we all knew the underlying issue. Even Maureen. And she was mortified."

Movement near the swinging kitchen doors caught my eye. It was the assistant manager. Her glasses slid down her nose and she pushed them back up, an annoyed look on her face. She still looked austere and uncomfortable in her skirt and high heels. But at least she'd lost the heavy blazer sometime during the night.

"What about her?" I asked.

"That's our assistant manager, Holly Barrows. She's pretty new. I think she started about six months ago."

"Do you usually have both an assistant manager and manager on the floor at the same time?" I asked.

Daisy nodded. "Holly comes in around three and stays until ten or so. Philippe always closed. He was in charge of handling the money and making sure everything was sound at night."

"She looks pretty shaken," I lied. She actually looked like she was angry and miserable. Of course, if I had to spend hours every night in heels, I'd be miserable, too.

"Holly heard Maureen scream and ran to see what was going on. So she also saw Philippe in his office dead."

Aunt Shirley tsked. "Poor girl. We should probably talk with her either tonight or tomorrow."

"Tomorrow," I said firmly.

Aunt Shirley gave me a wicked grin and shrugged. "We'll see."

"Daisy!" a curly-haired blonde called out, her hand motioning for Daisy.

"That's my friend. I guess she's done talking with the police. I better go."

"Thanks for the info," I said.

I watched her scurry over to her friend and accidentally made eye contact with Rod. He still looked pissed.

"Do you think it's as simple as Chef Benoit losing his temper and killing Philippe?" I asked Aunt Shirley.

26

She shrugged. "Could be. But then, it's rarely as simple as it looks."

I tore my gaze away from Rod and watched the detective in charge amble over our way.

"Ladies, sorry to keep you waiting."

I stared hard at the detective that had captured Aunt Shirley's attention. I had to admit, I didn't see the attraction for Aunt Shirley. He'd obviously been too long on the job and it showed. His once-toned body had gone soft in the middle over the years, and he sported a thick set of jowls that reminded me of a bulldog. His eyes, though still sharp, had probably been kind years ago, but now they held a cold hardness. Coupled with an unfortunate receding hairline, this man was not Aunt Shirley's usual eye candy.

"My name is Detective Dickerson, and I'm with the Las Vegas Metropolitan Police Station. I have a few questions I'd like to ask."

Aunt Shirley gasped.

From the quirked brow on Detective Dickerson's face, it was obvious he'd heard her, too.

"Dickie?" Aunt Shirley asked tentatively.

Detective Dickerson took a small step back and his mouth dropped open. "I haven't heard that name in years." He ran his eyes down Aunt Shirley…from the top of her head to the bottom of her feet. "You know, I've been trying to place you since the moment I saw you. I thought maybe you were one of the countless perps I've picked up over the years. But obviously it's more than that." His bushy eyebrows shot up. "I just can't place where I know you."

Aunt Shirley chuckled. "It's been a good many years since we've seen each other. I knew you when you were fresh out of the academy at the tender age of twenty. I was a seasoned PI having been on the job nearly ten years by then. But the Los Angeles Police Department would sometimes use me on their cases."

A huge grin nearly split Detective Dickerson's face in two. "Shirley Andrews? My gosh, how many years has it been?" He laughed self-consciously. "Never mind. Since I'm due to retire in a few months, I think I can answer that myself." He sobered instantly. "Do you live in Vegas? Are you still on the job? How're you involved in this case?"

Aunt Shirley beamed and slapped me on the back. "This here is my niece, Ryli, and we're in Vegas for her bachelorette party. We ate here earlier, and we were walking by when we saw the cops. So we thought we should stop on by. See, my niece saw Chef Benoit and the guy who died, this Philippe Bernard, fighting in the kitchen tonight."

"Uh-huh. And out of the goodness of your heart you thought you should wait around and maybe talk with other witnesses and get their perspective?"

Aunt Shirley said nothing…just grinned.

Detective Dickerson shook his head, his eyes twinkling. "You haven't changed a bit, Miss Shirley. Still itching to solve crimes even after all these years?"

"You know it, Dickie."

"Hey, come by Las Vegas Metro tomorrow, would you? I'd love to show you around to all the guys. They've heard enough about you over the years."

Aunt Shirley blushed. "I'd love nothing more!"

CHAPTER 5

"I still can't get over the fact that you know the lead detective for this case," I mused as I leaned against the wall of the restaurant.

Aunt Shirley closed her eyes momentarily. "Ole Dickie was a good egg. He was so squeaky clean and new when he got hired on with the LAPD. His partner and I were on and off lovers over the years, and I actually helped solve a lot of crimes in their precinct. I know I've told you that I sometimes worked as a consultant when my PI business was slow."

"I mean, I knew you said you did, but sometimes—well, let's be honest. Sometimes you tend to do a little Aunt Shirley exaggeration."

"Bite you tongue, kid." Aunt Shirley straightened and pushed herself off the wall. "Look over there. That waitress, Maureen, looks like she's done being questioned and going to the bathroom. Let's go make a pit stop ourselves."

Oh, yay. Bathroom interrogation. My favorite.

I sighed but followed like a puppy behind Aunt Shirley. A part of me was tired and ready to call it a night...the other part of me knew I should sit down and buckle up because I was about to go for a ride.

Maureen was splashing water on her swollen face when we walked into the bathroom. She made no comment to us as we entered, but her eyes did track our every movement. I could tell she was curious.

"Maureen? My name is Shirley Andrews and this is my niece, Ryli. We just wanted to say we're very sorry for your loss."

Tears fell from Maureen's eyes again, and I wanted to kick myself and Aunt Shirley for breaking this poor girl's heart. "Thank you. It was awful." Her voice was rough and dry from all the crying. She cleared it. "I'll never get the image out of my head."

I figured she was still half in shock. She didn't know us from Adam. There was no reason for her to be spilling her guts to us. Other than I knew from personal experience that sometimes it was good to talk about tragedy and get it out. Otherwise it would eat at you.

"Can you tell me what happened?" Aunt Shirley asked.

Maureen blinked a couple times as though trying to clear her mind. "Are you two with the police?"

I gave Aunt Shirley a hard look. I hated it when she lied.

"Not exactly," Aunt Shirley hedged. "Although I was in the business for about forty years. And I personally know Detective Dickerson."

"Oh, okay. What did you want to know?"

Maureen suddenly swayed and I caught her in my arms.

"You must be exhausted," I said. "Do you have a way to get home?"

She nodded, a blush spreading across her cheeks. "Chef Benoit said he'd take me home when this was over."

"Good," Aunt Shirley said firmly. "Now, can you tell us what happened?"

I stepped back when Maureen stopped swaying. "Like I told Detective Dickerson, I went to Philippe's office to let him know we had a customer asking to meet the Chef. We get that request a lot from our customers. Of course, Chef Benoit can't come out for every request, so our policy is to get the manager and have him smooth things over with the customer."

"Was Philippe's door open or closed?" Aunt Shirley asked.

"Closed." Maureen swiped at the tears that were once again falling from her eyes. "Which was odd. Usually Philippe left it open. It's a pretty cramped office…right off where the bussers usually deposit their dishes." Her voice hitched but she pushed on. "Philippe was sitting behind the desk, hunched over with duct tape across his mouth and wrists. I ran over to where he was sitting, and that's when—"

She broke off and covered her hands with her face. I reached over and gathered her in my arms and let her sob for a few minutes. When she was spent, she eased slowly out of my arms.

"I'm sorry," Maureen said softly. "It's just so awful when I picture it."

"It's okay," I said gently. "Can you tell us what you saw?"

Maureen took a deep breath. "His leg had been cut really bad. Like there was blood everywhere on his lower body." She wiped her eyes again. "I guess I was screaming, because Holly came rushing in. And that's when I saw that the knife had been dropped on the floor."

I groaned. "Did you pick it up?"

"I did! I honestly wasn't thinking at the time. I just saw it there and I picked it up."

Oh, Maureen. Either the dumbest move or a very clever move.

"When I told Chef Benoit what I'd done, he told me not to worry about it. Probably the killer either used gloves or even wiped off the knife so they'd never get fingerprints anyway." Maureen started shaking again. "But now *my* fingerprints are on the weapon!"

Aunt Shirley gave me a hard look even though she spoke to Maureen. "Chef Benoit is right. The killer probably did use gloves or wipe his or her fingerprints off the knife handle."

I knew what she was telling me. I didn't like anything about that scenario. If Maureen really was innocent and Chef Benoit killed Philippe, then he basically just set up his girlfriend to take the fall. Of course, he had no way of knowing who would go in there to discover the body. Unless he wanted to frame her to get back at her for fooling around with Philippe if the rumors were to be believed.

Oh, what a tangled web we weave.

31

"Please don't take this the wrong way, dear," Aunt Shirley said. "But you seem to be taking this really hard. Were you involved with Philippe?"

I heard Maureen's small gasp as she slid her gaze to the right. "Oh no. Workers aren't allowed to fraternize with each other."

We both stared knowingly at Maureen. Once again her face turned a light shade of pink and she started gnawing on her bottom lip.

"I'm being truthful when I say I wasn't seeing Philippe," Maureen said lamely.

So you're seeing Chef Benoit.

"But there's something you aren't telling us," Aunt Shirley insisted.

Maureen sighed. "I know how it probably looked to others, but the reason I'd been spending time with Philippe was because he was trying to talk me into going back to school. He thought I should get a degree in restaurant management. He said my personality would be a good fit for managing a restaurant. But it was our little secret."

"No one knew you were thinking about going to school?" I asked.

Maureen shook her head. "No. I wasn't convinced, so every chance he got, Philippe would brag about me to others. He was really pressuring me."

"Did he want you to manage here?" Aunt Shirley asked.

Maureen's brows furrowed and she grew very still. "No. We already have an assistant manager. I think he just wanted me to expand myself and do more. He knew…" Her voice trailed off.

"He knew what, dear?" Aunt Shirley prompted.

Maureen sighed. "Even though it's forbidden, he knew about me and Chef Benoit. I think he thought maybe if I elevated my job position, it would be easier for the two of us."

"But neither you nor Philippe ever told Chef Benoit what you were thinking about doing? Going back to management school?"

Maureen shook her head. "No. Like I said, Philippe had been pressuring me, but I hadn't fully committed."

So all Chef Benoit sees is you two hanging out together.

"Are there cameras near his office?" I asked.

"No. We have cameras in the main dining room, and a camera in the kitchen because we have a back door that leads to the outside."

"If we have any more questions, can we contact you?" Aunt Shirley asked.

Maureen blinked in surprise. "Of course."

I pulled out my cell phone and Maureen rattled off her number. We promised her we'd stop by again soon to see how things were going.

There was still a number of staff leaning against the walls when we exited the restroom and headed out of the restaurant.

"I can't get over this night," I said. "We have a con man scamming women, you reconciled with someone you haven't seen in years, and we have an unsolved murder. And we haven't even touched on anything remotely related to my bachelorette party."

Aunt Shirley grinned. "It's definitely been a good night."

We strolled past a long wall with myriad posters all advertising the fabulous and diverse entertainment the hotel provided. There were dozens of high-quality boutiques, an art gallery, and even a spa. One poster touted the prowess and dexterity of a group of half-naked performers swinging on silken ropes and large hooped circles. They promised to take the audience past their comfort zone and cross over into the taboo.

I don't think so.

Another poster had a magician dressed head to toe in black in the foreground with a knowing smirk on his face. In the background, a pretty, overly teased and hairsprayed blonde in a skimpy outfit stood inside a tall glass booth. The poster promised that Magician Harry Blackbourn and his lovely assistant would captivate their audience with daring escapes and illusions.

Too cheesy.

The last poster nearly made me pee. The hotel we were staying in was about twenty stories high—roughly two hundred feet in the air. Daunting enough on its own. But the hotel also boasted an amusement-park ride on their roof. This one went another two hundred feet up as the riders faced outward so they could see the city around them, and then suddenly the ride dropped you straight down.

Not only no...but hell no!

"Please tell me none of those things are on the to-do list for my bachelorette trip," I said as we stepped inside the elevator.

I pushed our floor number and waited for a response. When I didn't get one, I groaned. "I'm not riding that monstrous contraption on the roof. I'm also not—"

"You'll do what I say. I'm the one in charge of your party."

I narrowed my eyes at Aunt Shirley but said nothing. She was right. Not only was she in charge, but she graciously offered to pay for everything.

I should have known this would come back and bite me in the butt.

CHAPTER 6

"I can't believe you found a dead body," Garrett sighed wearily into the phone the next morning when I called. "I should have known this wouldn't go without a kink of some kind."

I scowled at my reflection in the bedroom mirror. "I didn't *find* a dead body. I just happened to be in a place that had a dead body discovered. And I'd talked to the guy that was murdered earlier that night. That's all."

Garrett bit back a laugh. "That's not all. You and I both know it. I suppose Aunt Shirley has convinced you to look into the murder?"

Didn't take much convincing. If you want to know the truth.

"I bet your poor mother is fit to be tied," Garrett continued.

"Mom wasn't happy when I told her this morning," I conceded.

Garrett sighed. "I'm not angry at you, Ryli. I just wish you could get away for some fun without tripping over dead bodies wherever you go."

"You and I both know I'm a magnet for trouble."

Garrett laughed. "You are. And I suppose it's one of the things I love about you. No matter how crazy the situation, you're right there ready to tackle it head on."

"So you still love me?" I asked sweetly.

"You know I do. You're my heart, and I can't wait to see you back here safely. If you need me, you'll call, right?"

"Of course," I lied.

"You're lying."

I smiled. "I love you, Garrett. I gotta run."

I hung up my cell and shoved it into my purse before walking out into the living room of the suite. Paige, Mom, and Mindy were watching TV while Aunt Shirley was pacing by the door.

"Finally," Aunt Shirley snapped.

I rolled my eyes. "We have plenty of time to get to the café without being late."

I strolled over and gave Mom a kiss on the cheek. "We won't be long. Let's try and meet up sometime soon."

Mom looked up at me and frowned. "I'm still a little upset over all this. First you meet a bunch of women and offer to help them out, and then you happen to stumble upon a dead body in the very restaurant we ate. How is it these things happen to you?"

"That seems to be the sixty-four-thousand-dollar question," I quipped. "Garrett just asked me the same thing. You both always do."

Mom sighed. "I love you. You two be careful and we'll catch up later."

I strode next to Aunt Shirley down the hallway to the elevator. I was still feeling a little guilty for making Garrett worry about me since I was so far away.

The elevator doors opened and we walked into the large entertainment and food service area of the hotel. Dozens of people were milling around looking at the posters and hitting up the boutiques.

"Look," Aunt Shirley said as she pointed to the yellow tape in front of the restaurant we ate at last night. "Looks like they're still closed down."

"They don't have to open for dinner until around four. Think the tape will be down by then?"

Aunt Shirley shook her head. "Nope. But they should be open by Friday. We'll have to come back then and snoop around."

I grinned. "Oh yeah."

"That's my girl."

36

We walked farther down the enormous tiled walkway until we came to the café. Aunt Shirley nudged my arm and pointed to the group of women sitting at a circular table. "There they are."

"There's three of them now," I hissed. "Ole Arthur must really be making the rounds."

I'm not sure why, but the thought of a sleazy old man ripping off nice old ladies really had my blood boiling. I wanted to believe that little old men were all like Old Man Jenkins. He was such a gentleman. He'd never think to dupe nice ladies out of money and jewelry.

A hush fell over the table as Aunt Shirley and I pulled out our chairs and sat down.

"I went by Eleanor's room this morning to see how things went," Cheryl Owens started off. "Needless to say, I found a weeping Eleanor."

A sob caught in Eleanor's throat and she dabbed her eyes with her napkin. "I can't believe I was such a fool."

"What's missing?" Aunt Shirley demanded.

Eleanor didn't say anything at first. Her thin, bluish lips were pressed together so hard I was afraid she might dislocate her jaw. "My deceased husband's pinky ring. It's a square gold piece with a small diamond in the middle. I always carry it with me to keep him close." A tear slid down her cheek and she brushed it aside. "It just makes me sick thinking that he'll be wearing something my husband loved. How could he do something so heinous?"

My heart ached for her. I could clearly see the pain etched on her face, and I felt like I'd been sucker punched. I didn't care what it took, Arthur Tisdale was going down. Going down hard.

The waiter came by and took our order. An iced caramel mocha for me and a double espresso for Aunt Shirley. One of us intended on having a caffeine high by ten o'clock…and it wasn't me.

37

We spent the next twenty minutes going over our plan to not only get the girls' jewelry back, but to make sure Arthur Tisdale never messed with another woman again. I had to admit, Aunt Shirley could be very scary when she wanted to be.

"Are you sure you can do your part?" Cheryl asked me as she twisted her hands in her lap. "It sounds dangerous."

I had to agree. But I vowed to do whatever I could for these grieving women.

"I got this," I said, faking a bravado I didn't feel.

"I hope so," Mildred grumbled. "Otherwise we'll never get our stuff back."

I didn't know Mildred Biggins from Adam, but she already had a big strike against her. I'd met another Mildred months ago that lived at the Manor on the same floor as Aunt Shirley.

I despised her.

This Mildred was becoming a close second. There must be something about the name Mildred I didn't like.

"You hush up," Aunt Shirley snapped. "If my niece says she can do it, then she can do it." Even though everyone else heard Aunt Shirley stick up for me...I heard the underlying threat in her voice. If I messed this up, Aunt Shirley'd personally kick my butt herself.

Cheryl laid a hand over Mildred's arm. "We trust you both explicitly. If you say you can get our things back, then I believe you can. We're just so grateful for your help."

"Yes," Eleanor quickly added. "I can't go home with my husband's ring missing. If my children were to find out, it would be the last straw."

I furrowed my brow. "What do you mean?"

Eleanor took a deep, shaky breath then let it out slowly. "I've become somewhat of a burden lately to my children, and they've been threatening for a few months now to put me in a home. Not one of those nice assisted living facilities...but an actual nursing home!"

Aunt Shirley and I both gasped. It was one thing for active people in their seventies to live in hip, fun assisted living establishments like the one Aunt Shirley lived in. Once you reach a certain age, a lot of people don't want to have to worry about taking care of a yard or throwing money away on a house that's falling down around them. But it's a whole other thing to be discarded by your own family in a full-blown nursing home when you were still vibrant and active.

"We won't let that happen," I promised Eleanor.

No matter what, I'd get the jewelry back for these women. I just hoped it didn't end with me getting arrested. Garrett would so frown on me getting an arrest record on my bachelorette trip with the girls.

I mean, he wouldn't exactly be surprised…he'd just frown *a lot* and lecture me *a lot*.

"The seniors are all going to a haunted mine shaft where they let you pan for gold and talk to ghosts," Cheryl said. "So we won't be home until late tonight. You may have to do the first part of your plan on Friday night. Would that be okay?"

"No problem," Aunt Shirley said.

***

"I'm really proud of the way you've been stepping up," Aunt Shirley said as we sat down at two empty slot machines next to Paige.

I'd called up to the room after we left the ladies in the café to see if Paige, Mindy, and Mom were up to playing some slots. Mom and Mindy were out shopping, but Paige was available.

"What do you mean?" I asked.

"I mean the way you've been asking more questions, paying attention to your surroundings, taking in the actions and emotions of the perps all around you."

A Burning Hot Murder

A year ago, had Aunt Shirley said that to me, I'd have thrown a fit and lectured her on not getting me involved in trouble. Now I find myself embracing it more and more. I really *did* want to help those women. I really *did* want to find out what happened to Philippe, the manager that'd been murdered.

"Maybe you should go into the PI business," Paige giggled as she pulled down the lever and watched her slot spin. She was an old-fashioned player. She wanted to pull the lever, not push a button to activate the machine. "Could you imagine? Garrett would *die!*"

I started to laugh.

Then stopped.

Was that *really* a stupid idea? Yes. Yes, it was. Garrett wanted to start a family soon. It's not like I could chase down bad guys nine months pregnant.

"Oh, no!" Paige cried. "I know that look. No way, Ryli. No way!"

Aunt Shirley let out a war whoop and clapped her hands together. "Hell yeah! Now you're thinkin' girl! We could go into business together." Aunt Shirley got a glassy look in her eye, gasped, and slowly arced her hand in front of her. "I got it! I got the slogan. 'Need our help? Just ask. We're Andrews, Sinclair-Kimble. All you need to do is ask.' Get it! Our initials are ASK. It's perfect!"

It is *perfect!*

I closed my eyes and breathed deeply. I had to get a grasp on reality. The problem with Aunt Shirley is that being around her was intoxicating and fun. Of course, the next day you're left with a severe hangover and wondering what you did and how you got the tattoo you're currently sporting. That was life with Aunt Shirley.

"No, no. I can't do something like that," I said. "I'm about to get married, start a family. Besides, we already have jobs with Hank. What're we gonna do, quit our jobs as reporters?"

40

Aunt Shirley pursed her lips. "Well, I suppose we would have to keep those jobs for now. But maybe we could get enough clients from the bigger cities like Brywood and Kansas City who could use our help."

I was grasping at straws now. "I'm not even sure the route you'd have to take to even become a private investigator in Missouri."

Aunt Shirley smirked. "You need to be twenty-one, fingerprinted and pass a background check, get general liability insurance, and take a two-hour licensing exam. The exam is given every Tuesday in Jefferson City. You'll find out that day if you passed."

"Holy crap," I said. "That's it?"

"Ryli Jo Sinclair," Paige huffed. "You need to stop thinking about such foolishness. You're going to get married, have a baby, and live happily ever after with Garrett. Stop this nonsense talk." She rubbed her hand over her massive belly. "You're upsetting the twins."

I tried to laugh because I knew that's what she expected...but I suddenly couldn't breathe. I couldn't get air, I couldn't swallow, my vision was getting spotty, and I thought I was going to keel over.

"Get your head down between your legs," Aunt Shirley demanded as she turned my chair to face outward. I must not have complied fast enough because I felt Aunt Shirley's hand on my back. "You're having a panic attack."

"Why am I having a panic attack?" I mumbled between my legs. This was so not an appropriate position to be in while in public.

Aunt Shirley pushed me back up into a sitting position and gave Paige the stink eye. "Because someone is projecting *her* lifestyle onto you and you aren't having it."

I laid my arm on Aunt Shirley's. "Paige didn't mean anything by it. She's right. It's always been my dream to get

41

married and have kids. Or at least it was. Now I'm not sure what I want. I mean, I want Garrett. I want to be married to him." I turned to Aunt Shirley, tears filling my eyes. "I want that more than anything. I love him so much."

"I know, dear." Aunt Shirley continued patting my hand. "But there's also nothing wrong with your dreams changing."

I turned to look at Paige. I could tell she was scared to death. If the pale skin didn't give it away, the open mouth and tears in her eyes did. "I thought marriage and babies was what you wanted, Ryli. I'm sorry."

What's wrong with me?

"It *is* what I want. Although, I've been having a lot of doubt lately. I mean, I've always doubted my ability in being good at marriage. I don't cook, clean, or really do anything domestic very well. And motherhood scares me to death."

Paige giggled. "Ryli, we all have those doubts. I did."

I blinked in surprise. "You did?"

"Yes. But eventually my fears subsided and I've come to realize I love being married to your brother, and I'm kinda good at it. I'm good for him. Just like you're good for Garrett."

"The knocked-up girl has a point," Aunt Shirley said. "You'll be great at marriage and family. I'm just saying you don't have to give up your dreams *solely* because you got married and started a family."

Could I honestly have both? Would Garrett honestly be okay if I started a new adventure right when we get married?

"Just something to think about," Aunt Shirley said. "No one is saying you have to go out and get a PI license when we get home. I'm just saying you're good at what you do. It took me many years on the job to get as good as you've gotten in just one year."

I laughed bitterly. "That's because we can't help but stumble over dead bodies everywhere."

"That's true." Aunt Shirley took a deep breath. "I need to tell you something."

The seriousness in her voice had me instantly on guard. "What?"

"It hasn't just been one time I asked Old Man Jenkins for help. About a month ago I had him take me to Brywood to be fingerprinted."

Warning bells went off in my head. "Why?"

"I didn't want Garrett to find out just in case something went wrong."

"What have you done?" I asked.

"I know what's required for a private investigator because I was notified before we left Missouri the other day that I passed the background check. I'm due to take the exam the following week we get back home."

"What?" Paige and I exclaimed.

Aunt Shirley held up her hand. "Listen, you're moving on with your life, and I thought maybe I might start practicing again."

I snapped my mouth closed before I started catching flies. "You can't drive. How're you going to get to jobs?"

Aunt Shirley shrugged. "I don't know. All I know is that everyone is moving on with their life, and I don't want to stand still."

I winced at her words. She was right. Instead of tearing her down I should be building her up. It had to be hard to see everything change around her.

I started to laugh. "Mom is going to flip."

"Please, Garrett is going to nut out!" Paige exclaimed.

Aunt Shirley grinned. "Maybe I can get a job as a consultant with the Granville Police Department."

I laughed with her. "Yeah, and maybe you'll go to the Olympics as an ice skater."

Aunt Shirley shrugged. "Who know. But let's just keep this a secret between the three of us for right now. Deal?"

"Deal!" Paige and I said. Neither one of us wanted to be anywhere near the family when this cat gets let out of the bag.

"Let's play a couple more minutes," Aunt Shirley said. "Then I gotta head to the gym."

I frowned. "Why're you going to the hotel gym to work out instead of staying here and gambling with us?"

Aunt Shirley scoffed. "I'm not going to the gym to work out, you ninny."

Okay.

"I'm going to the gym because it's cheaper than going to a strip club. All those men in skimpy attire, sweating, panting, grunting, bending, stretching." Aunt Shirley fanned herself. "Whew!"

Paige and I doubled over. I laughed so hard I had tears in my eyes. I could hear Paige begging Aunt Shirley to stop. She was about to pee herself.

"And," Aunt Shirley continued, "I got my trusty alcohol-dispensing purse. So I can have a shot of tequila and enjoy the show. I'm just deciding if I should bring a couple ones or not."

"No!" I cried in horror. "It's one thing for you to go and look, it's another to actually *pay* the men in the gym. That will get you arrested!"

Aunt Shirley shrugged. "I'll play it by ear."

I turned back to my slot machine. There comes a time when you have to draw a line in the sand with Aunt Shirley. I was drawing the line.

I pulled down on the lever and watched as the wheel spun in front of me. The flashing lights and a little whistle caught my attention.

"You got a free spin!" Paige exclaimed.

"Yes!" I cried. "What does that mean?"

Aunt Shirley laughed. "It means you spin again and look up there at the top of the machine to see where the spinner stops. You win whatever it lands on."

I looked up and my breath caught. Those were high numbers! I grabbed the lever, held my breath, and watched the dial move across the numbers fast...then slower, and slower, and slower...until finally it stopped.

"Omigod!" I screamed. "It landed on two hundred!" I jumped out of my chair and did a little jig. Images of what I was going to do with my winnings flashed through my brain. Maybe I'd treat myself to a new outfit. Maybe I'd get Garrett that new gun he'd been hinting about. Two hundred extra dollars would definitely come in handy.

"What in tarnation are you getting so excited about?" Aunt Shirley asked.

I pointed to the number at the top of the slot machine and did a couple bobble head and hip gyrations. I decided that wasn't enough and sang my next couple sentences. "Because I won two hundred. Because I won two hundred. Don't be jealous...because I won two hundred."

I knew I shouldn't gloat too hard, but I couldn't help it. I could hear Paige laughing, but I figured she was just jealous of my smooth moves and massive win.

Aunt Shirley shook her head in disgust. "Do you even know what that means?"

I stopped dancing and looked at her incredulously. "Of course I know what it means. It means I just won two hundred smackers. Two hundred buckaroos. Two hundred clams."

Aunt Shirley shook her head in amazement. "You ninny! You're playing nickel slots. It means you won *two hundred nickels*! You're dancing and singing in public like an idiot for ten bucks!"

CHAPTER 7

"You sure you know where you're going in this thing?" Aunt Shirley asked for the fifth time in ten minutes.

"Yes! I pulled an app up that will get me to the police station. We only have a few more blocks."

After much grumbling, Mom had let me take her Tahoe to escort Aunt Shirley to the police station so she could meet up with Detective Dickerson. And to do some snooping on the restaurant murder…we weren't fooling anyone.

Aunt Shirley crossed her arms and sulked. "I still say we should have taken one of those Goobers and let someone chauffeur us around the city."

I rolled my eyes but didn't correct her ridiculous word. Let her think the word was Goober. I wasn't going to argue with her.

Aunt Shirley crossed her arms over her sagging chest. "It's gonna be embarrassing rolling up in the police station in a *Tahoe* instead of the Falcon. It's humiliating!"

"Would you give it a rest," I pleaded. "No one is going to give a rat's buttock what kind of car you're driving."

Aunt Shirley turned to glare at me. "This is Vegas. Everyone cares about what kind of car you're driving."

"How about I park waaaaay down the street and we walk five blocks so no one will see us?"

A little sarcastic, I know. But sometimes you had to be that way in order for Aunt Shirley to see how ridiculous she's being.

"Maybe," Aunt Shirley said.

I stand corrected.

"Think Detective Dickerson will let anything slip about the murder investigation and what all he's found out?" I asked, hoping

46

to divert her attention away from the fact she wasn't being driven around in the Falcon.

Aunt Shirley shrugged. "If he does, it will be deliberate...but it will come across as accidental. Legally he can't tell us anything, and I'm not a consultant."

I smiled slyly. "I like that. Deliberate, but sneaky."

I took a left at the street the mechanical voice inside my phone directed me to. The Las Vegas Metropolitan Police Department building had to be one of the largest stations I'd ever seen.

By the time we made it through and up to the homicide division, I didn't think there was a place left on my body that hadn't been probed or scanned. This place was definitely thorough.

We gave the man behind the counter our names and who we were there to see. A few minutes later Detective Dickerson came out to greet us.

"Shirley! Ryli! So nice to see you girls today."

Aunt Shirley all but giggled at the mention of her being a girl.

Laying it on a little thick, aren't ya, Dickerson?

"My niece and I had a little unfinished business this morning we needed to take care of before we came over, but we finally made it."

"Unfinished business?" Detective Dickerson quirked his eyebrow. "Anything I should know about?"

"Nothing I can't handle, Dickie."

Detective Dickerson laughed and patted Aunt Shirley on the back. "Still the same. Keeping everything close and not sharing anything."

Detective Dickerson stepped back and ushered us back toward his private office. Four other detectives were huddled around desks as we strode through the room. "Dias. Stow. Come over here and meet someone."

Two of the detectives looked up and made their way over to where we were standing. They were complete opposite of each other.

"Guys, I want you to meet someone special. This is Shirley Andrews, the private investigator lady I've talked about all these years."

A short, muscular man stuck out his hand. "My name's Ramon Dias. It's nice to meet you after all this time."

Aunt Shirley puffed out her chest. "Thank you. I was one of the best and often helped the Los Angeles Police Department out."

"That's what Dickerson's been telling us for years." The tall, blonde, Nordic-god stuck out his hand next. "Name's Michael Stow. And it's nice to meet you both."

I shook his hand and barely refrained from wincing. The man was definitely not someone I'd ever want to tangle with—in a darken alley or at high noon, it didn't matter.

Dias slapped Detective Dickerson on the back. "We're gonna miss this guy's stories when he retires shortly."

I'd never seen a cop blush before—I don't think Garrett even knows how to be embarrassed. It was rather appealing on Detective Dickerson.

"Well, we've got a lot of catching up to do. I just wanted you two to meet a very special lady." Detective Dickerson turned and ushered us into his private office. It was hardly bigger than a postage stamp. You definitely wanted to make sure you had your deodorant on before you squeezed into this box.

"I see the police tape is still up at the restaurant," Aunt Shirley said, diving straight into the real reason why we were here.

"Yep." Detective Dickerson's mouth twitched. He knew what Aunt Shirley was up to.

Aunt Shirley narrowed her eyes. "I guess since the fingerprints were on the murder weapon you'll probably arrest someone soon, right?"

Detective Dickerson shrugged. "I don't recall getting back all the information I need before making an arrest."

Aunt Shirley crossed her arms. "You and I both know that waitress Maureen had her hands all over the handle of that knife blade."

Detective Dickerson shook his head. "I can neither confirm nor deny that accusation."

"No need to confirm or deny anything," Aunt Shirley said slowly. "I spoke with Maureen last night. She told me her fingerprints were all over the murder weapon."

Detective Dickerson lifted one shoulder. "Could be then."

It was like watching a championship tennis match. One would talk, then the other. My head was like the quintessential bobble head being tossed about as they spoke.

"Have you already questioned the head Chef?" Aunt Shirley asked. "What's his name?"

"Chef Benoit," I supplied, glad to be contributing to this banter.

"Possibly," Detective Dickerson said.

Aunt Shirley frowned at Detective Dickerson. "Are you thinking of bringing him in for more formal questioning?"

Detective Dickerson said nothing, just tilted his head and lifted one shoulder.

The sudden rap on Detective Dickerson's door made me jump and let out a little scream. A handsome young cop in a neatly pressed uniform shuffled his feet outside Detective Dickerson's door. "Sir. Sorry to bother you." He sent inquisitive looks to Aunt Shirley and me. "But your next appointment is here."

"Thanks, Officer Mallon. Give me three minutes and then go ahead and send him on back."

Officer Mallon swallowed nervously and sent Aunt Shirley and me another glance.

"We're on our way out," Aunt Shirley assured Officer Mallon. She turned and picked up her huge purse off the chair.

"Right," Officer Mallon said. "I'll send Chef Keller back in three minutes."

Detective Dickerson shook his head as the officer headed back where he came from. "Kid's definitely still green. Imagine saying a witness's name in front of possible suspects for all he knows."

Aunt Shirley grinned. "I definitely don't know anyone who ever did that, Dickie."

Detective Dickerson's eyes softened at Aunt Shirley. "Those were some good times, Shirley." He turned his adoring gaze to me. "Your aunt was very patient when she had to work with me. I was constantly messing up like that boy just did, and she'd sternly chew me out."

I gave Aunt Shirley my best glare. "I hear ya, man. I feel your pain when it comes to trying to please this woman."

Aunt Shirley laughed good-naturedly. "It doesn't matter if I'm thirty-five or seventy-five, I'm still having to teach you youngins a thing or two. Will you be making an arrest soon?"

Detective Dickerson said nothing for a few seconds. "Let's just say, depending on how this session goes, and two other sessions I have later with potential witnesses, there might be something happening in this case."

"So you're looking pretty hard at Chef Benoit for the murder?" Aunt Shirley asked.

"Now, Shirley Andrews, you know I can't give you information on an on-going case." Detective Dickerson paused before adding, "But what I can say is that if you want to eat one of Chef Benoit's dishes again before you leave Las Vegas, you might have some trouble doing that."

Bingo! Aunt Shirley was right…very subtle.

Aunt Shirley grinned. "Thanks, Dickie!"

"No thanks needed. I didn't do anything." He winked at Aunt Shirley.

The three of us paused at the door and looked around. I was hoping for a glimpse of this Chef Keller person. Not that I knew who he was, but I thought maybe he might look familiar to me.

The Vegas sun was bright and hot when we finally reached the main entrance of the massive building. I reached inside my purse and shoved sunglasses on my face before starting on the trek back to the Tahoe.

"Looks like Chef Benoit is their main suspect," I said as I pulled the Tahoe out onto the street. "Is he yours?"

Aunt Shirley didn't say anything for a few seconds. "No. He's really not. I don't know why, but I'm not liking him for the murder."

"Even though he has the most to gain from Philippe being dead?"

Aunt Shirley grinned. "We only *assume* he had the most to gain. We don't know for sure. And you know what they say about assuming anything."

I rolled my eyes but said nothing.

The streets were busy as cars rushed to beat the traffic lights. I was lost in my own world when I felt Aunt Shirley pounding on my arm.

"Ouch! Stop hitting me. I'm driving!"

"Turn around! Turn around! Do you have any idea who that is that just passed us?"

I looked in my rearview mirror at the tail end of a funky looking car. "Nope. Not a clue."

Aunt Shirley was pulling at her pink and purple tuffs. "I can't believe he didn't turn around! This is the kind of car he goes gaga over. What's the matter with him?"

I furrowed my brow as I stopped at the next light. "That guy likes Tahoes?"

Aunt Shirley gave me a disgusted look. "No, he loves classic cars like—" She broke off with a sharp gasp and looked around as if taking in her surroundings for the first time. "I'm not in the Falcon!"

"Wow, Aunt Shirley, nothing gets by you," I said dryly.

"Turn this car around. We'll chase him down."

I laughed sardonically. "I'm not turning the car around, and I'm definitely not chasing down a complete stranger."

Aunt Shirley turned her blazing eyes on me. *"TURN THIS CAR AROUND!"*

I swear, the voice that came out of her was *not* human.

I made an illegal U-turn when the light turned green. I didn't see the classic car in front of me anywhere. "I don't see him."

"Keep driving. Keep looking." Aunt Shirley whipped out a tube of lipstick and began applying while I swiveled my head back and forth along the side streets.

"Who exactly are we looking for?" I asked.

"The Count! He's such a stud muffin!"

"The Count? What is he, titled royalty or a vampire?"

I laughed at my own joke...until Aunt Shirley's face took on a dangerously red hue. "Don't ever joke about my man like that!"

"I thought Old Man Jenkins was your man?"

Aunt Shirley snorted as she went back to looking up and down the side streets. "I'd drop that old man like a hot potato if the Count made a play at me!"

"I didn't get a good look, but the guy in the car looked pretty young compared to you."

Aunt Shirley pushed up her sagging chest. "He is. But I'd be willing to teach him a few tricks."

I gagged. "Look, I don't see the car anywhere. I'm sorry. But I don't know these streets so I don't want to veer off too far."

Aunt Shirley sighed. "I know his shop is over on Highland Drive, but since he's in a car driving around, there's no sense going over there to catch a glimpse."

She sounded so dejected, I couldn't help but feel sorry for her. "I'm sorry, Aunt Shirley. Maybe we can stop by this shop of his while we're still in town and see if you can't see him again."

She lifted one shoulder. "Maybe." She suddenly brightened. "Or maybe we come back to Vegas when we're in the Falcon. Then if we didn't see him on the streets we could stop by the shop and he'd talk with us!"

I didn't have the heart to tell her the chance of that happening was slim to none. Not so much that he wouldn't talk with us…but the simple truth of the matter being that once I got married, my spontaneous girl trips would probably dissipate.

I wasn't sure what to make of the hollow feeling in my heart.

"We need to cheer up," I said. "Let's go back and get the girls and gamble a little. With the restaurant closed *and* the seniors on their haunted mine trip, tonight should be a pretty slow night for us."

Aunt Shirley brightened. "It *is* Thirsty Thursday. Perhaps we should pay homage?"

I laughed. "Sure, why not."

CHAPTER 8

"I'm so glad we're all going to the restaurant again tonight," I said as I took the glass of champagne Paige offered me. "I couldn't believe it when I walked by earlier today and the yellow tape was down and a sign said they'd be open tonight. I'm curious to see what's going on after Wednesday night's murder."

"Ryli Jo," Mom said exasperatingly. "I don't want you getting mixed up in this murder. This is your bachelorette weekend. You will not be spending it solving a murder that doesn't concern you. Do you understand me?"

"Oh, of course," I assured Mom. Not the least bit meaning it. And, no surprise, she didn't believe me when I said it.

"I mean it," Mom reiterated. "No more investigating."

I took a long swallow of the drink so I didn't have to answer her. I figured I was good since I didn't exactly lie to her.

"I can't wait to see the magic show tonight," Mindy said by way of changing the subject.

"Me, too," Paige said excitedly. "I've heard these Vegas shows are spectacular."

Aunt Shirley laughed as I groaned. "We're pretty much doing verything Ryli told me she didn't want to do. I'm the aunt, I get to t the rules."

I rolled my eyes but didn't say anything. Mainly because she ˙ right. If she wanted to take me to see that creepy guy and his ˙pily clad blonde assistant, who was I to rain on her parade.

We made our way to the elevator, talking incessantly about we thought the magic show would entail. Our spirits were ˙ we hurried into the restaurant. We were a little early for dinner—the restaurant having opened five minutes ago—but I was hoping to catch Maureen. I didn't figure too many people would be looking to eat dinner at four o'clock, especially when a murder had taken place in said restaurant two nights before.

"Welcome," the maître d said in a haughty voice. "Do you prefer a booth or table?"

"Actually," I said, "could we sit in Maureen's section?"

The maître d lifted one arched brow even higher. "So you've dined with us before?"

"Wednesday night," Aunt Shirley said smugly.

I caught the surprised look on the maître d's face. "Oh, well, welcome back. If you'll follow me, I'll seat you in Maureen's section."

There was an awkward silence as we followed him to our table. There were only a few other couples in the restaurant.

"This is Maureen's section," he said, handing us our sheet of paper. "Bon appétit."

The maître d scurried off before I could ask him any questions. Not that I had questions ready. Besides, he didn't look familiar. He wasn't the guy that sat us Wednesday night.

"Hello. My name is Maureen, and I'll be your—"

Maureen broke off when she recognized us. Her breath caught and she took an involuntary step backward. Her eyes wide as she looked over her shoulder at the kitchen.

"Hi, Maureen," I said as jovially as I could. "Do you remember my aunt and me?"

Maureen swallowed hard, her throat moving with the force. "Yes. From Wednesday night."

"I was surprised to see the police let you open up the restaurant today." I wanted to put her at ease.

Maureen nodded. "The police called Holly around two and said we could open tonight. They were finished collecting all the evidence."

"How're you holding up, dear?" Aunt Shirley asked.

Maureen's lower lip trembled and tears filled her eyes. "Actually, not very well. I'm terribly worried about Chef." She bit her lip and stopped speaking.

"Have you heard anything more from Detective Dickerson today?" Aunt Shirley prodded.

Maureen shook her head. She whipped out her order booklet and asked us what we wanted to drink. We gave her our drink order, and with a promise to be back soon, she turned and fled.

"I find it a little odd no one has heard from Dickie today," Aunt Shirley said. "I thought for sure he'd be here making an arrest. Or at least a lengthy detainment. Guess Dickie is slacking on his job."

"Shirley Andrews!" Mom chastised. "It's not nice calling him that vile name."

Aunt Shirley chuckled. "I've known Dickie forever. Believe me, he embraces the name."

We spent the next few minutes looking over the sheet of paper to figure out what we wanted to eat. Maureen had been so flustered she'd forgot to tell us the specials. I was still vacillating between the sea bass or the boeuf bourguignon when she returned with our drinks. I'd ordered the French Kiss—white crème de cacao, orange vodka, and grated orange. Not exactly a good pairing for either meal choice, but there was still plenty of time for wine.

I caught movement out of the corner of my eye and turned to see Detective Dickerson and three uniformed police officers barrel their way into the kitchen. Chaos erupted seconds later.

"No!" Maureen cried, her hand flying to cover her open mouth.

"Who are they arresting?" Mindy asked.

Maureen doubled over as if in pain. I was about to grab hold of her when the assistant manager, Holly Barrows, charged out of the kitchen and headed straight for Maureen.

"No!" Maureen cried again as the young manager grabbed hold of Maureen's arm.

"I'm sorry to interrupt your dinner," Holly said dismissively. "Maureen, if you can come with me, please. We have an emergency in the back."

"Is everything okay?" Aunt Shirley demanded.

"Everything is fine, ladies. Please enjoy your meal."

She obviously didn't recognize Aunt Shirley or me from Wednesday night. I got a feeling this could work in our favor. We might be able to move about freely if we could distract Holly.

Holly dragged Maureen off toward the kitchen, and I turned to Aunt Shirley. "Think they're arresting Chef Benoit tonight?"

"Looks that way." Aunt Shirley took a sip of her Parisian Paradise—an absinthe and vermouth concoction with sugar, bitters, and orange peel. "God that's good."

I stole a glance at Mom. I could tell by the way her lips were pinched together, she knew what I was about to say and she wasn't happy.

"I bet if you girls snuck back in the kitchen after the police come out," Mindy said nonchalantly, "you could find out what's going on."

I didn't know whether to laugh or kiss Mindy. The woman could read a situation like no one's business. She knew if I made the proposition, Mom would immediately object. But if *she* made the suggestion, maybe it wouldn't seem so dangerous.

Mom sighed. "I really don't want Ryli involved."

"She's already involved," Aunt Shirley said. "You can't stop the inevitable from happening."

Paige rested a hand on Mom's forearm. "Aunt Shirley is right. This is what they do. Let them get this out of their system, then we can continue with dinner and the magic show."

I nodded enthusiastically and held up my hand. "I promise. If you distract Holly for us, Aunt Shirley and I will run back and see what we can find out. We won't mention the murder again for the rest of the night. Scout's honor."

Mom chuckled. "You were never a scout, Ryli Jo."

I hid my smile behind my drink.

I was saved from a response when the kitchen's swinging doors flew open and Chef Benoit, handcuffed and sputtering, was being shoved along by Detective Dickerson. One of the uniformed cops reading Chef Benoit his rights.

"Wow," I said. "I didn't expect an arrest so soon, and in so public of a way. Maybe they'd have him come down to the station again for questioning, but a full-on arrest...surprising."

Aunt Shirley frowned. "Something tells me there's more here. Dickie looks like he's swallowed a hot pepper. His face is all contorted and red. I bet it started out as a request for questioning, but Chef Benoit protested a little too much and got himself arrested."

I downed my French Kiss and wiggled my eyebrows at Aunt Shirley. "Let's go find out."

Aunt Shirley grinned. "Now you're talking."

"Please be careful," Mom admonished as Aunt Shirley and I rose from the table.

"If they come to take our order," I said, "I'll take the beef bourguignon with..." I trailed off when I looked at the wine they suggested to pair with the meal. No way in heck was I gonna be able to pronounce that.

I pointed to the wine I wanted. "That one right there."

Mom scoffed. "I can't pronounce that!"

"Just point to it," I said. "I'm sure these people are used to that."

Aunt Shirley and I slowly made our way toward the kitchen. I could feel Mom's eyes on my back the whole way.

When we got to the swinging doors, Aunt Shirley pulled me back against the wall, then pushed open the doors a fraction of an inch.

"I can't believe this!" Holly Barrows cried. "Who's going to take his place?"

I heard a man clear his throat. "That would be me, Holly. As Sous Chef, I'm next in line."

"I know that!" Holly snapped. "I know how to do my job!"

"No one said otherwise, Holly," Maureen soothed. "We're all just a little upset over what's happened." Her voice hitched on the last word and seconds later I could hear sobbing.

"Patty, take Maureen to your station and get her calmed down," Holly commanded. "I'll go back out and see to her tables. I'm sure the guests are beside themselves over this spectacle."

I turned, grabbed Aunt Shirley, and together we fled down by the restrooms. I hoped it would look like we were walking out if someone saw us.

Holly stopped and frowned. "Can I help you with something?"

"Oh, no," I said quickly. "We just needed to use the restroom, and we're hoping to order soon."

Holly's nostril's flared. "I'll be right there to take your order."

"Is everything okay?" Aunt Shirley asked. "We saw the police hauling away one of your chefs."

Holly smoothed her palms down over her short, brown skirt. Tonight her hair wasn't pulled back in a severe bun. Instead, it was gathered in a loose slip knot at the top of her head. And instead of the long-sleeved blazer, she wore a button-up white shirt. She looked less threatening and more approachable tonight.

"Everything is fine. The police just needed to question our chef a little more. But don't worry, our Sous Chef, Marcus Keller, is cooking for us tonight. Guaranteed to be spectacular. Chef Keller has trained with Chef Benoit for years now, and has been waiting with baited breath to finally take the reins. Looks like tonight he will get his shot."

Now I know who Chef Keller is.

All sorts of alarms and whistles went off in my head. Could Chef Keller have murdered Philippe Bernard and set up his boss, Chef Benoit, just to take over as head chef? When I thought about it, it didn't seem too far a stretch.

"It's good to know Chef Keller can step in and fill Chef Benoit shoes," Aunt Shirley said.

"When it's your time, it's your time," Holly said as she stepped around us and made her way farther into the restaurant.

What had she meant by that?

"What the heck did that mean?" Aunt Shirley demanded.

I shrugged. "Who knows. How're we gonna find where Patty's station is? Is she a server or another chef?"

Aunt Shirley grinned. "Everyone is gonna be so worked up over cooking with a new chef and the old chef being arrested. Most of them won't even look twice at us."

I wasn't so sure, but we stealthily crept back to the swinging doors, careful not to get hit. Aunt Shirley peeked in the round window, her head swiveling back and forth to take in the whole kitchen, then flattened back against the wall. "Looks like the servers are up front here, while the chefs are more toward the back of the restaurant. There's a section off to the right that's separated from the rest of the kitchen. A woman chef is standing there, glaring at Maureen from across the kitchen. We're gonna creep in nice and silent, stick to the wall, and go talk with the menacing female chef. Maureen is up front talking with—I'm assuming—this Patty girl. I only saw three other servers in the front, and one was texting on her phone while the others were talking with each other. Hopefully they won't notice us."

I swallowed hard and nodded. We had to do this to get more information, otherwise we'd be at a stalemate. I learned long ago that just because the police think someone did it, doesn't mean it's always a slam dunk.

Aunt Shirley pushed open the left side of the swinging door and slid immediately to her right. I followed close behind and took a quick look at my surroundings. Aunt Shirley had been right. Since the restaurant had just opened, there wasn't a need for a large serving staff right now. The four women were occupied and didn't pay us any attention.

I averted my gaze and stared at the wall as Aunt Shirley and I crept quickly to where the female chef was standing near the right-hand side of the massive kitchen.

There were two counters filled with Eclairs, an apple tart, chocolate mousse, crème brûlée, and myriad other desserts. Embracing my new role as a detective, I went ahead and surmised that since the woman was wearing a hat and white coat, she must be a pastry chef or something.

"What're you two doing back here?" she growled when she saw us. "You can't be back here. You need to leave. Now!"

CHAPTER 9

Even though the woman had been growling at us, she never once gave us more than a cursory glance. Instead, she continued to glare ice daggers at Maureen.

"Chef Quinn, I'm going to load the cart." A perky, curly-haired girl said as she gave Aunt Shirley and me an inquisitive look.

The pastry chef snapped out of her glaring trance and scowled at the girl. "Fine. Just make sure you do it correctly this time. Don't forget to get the lemon soufflé out of the back kitchen."

The girl's cheeks turned pink as she tilted her head. "Of course, Chef Quinn." She scurried past us and started loading the succulent desserts onto a cart. I suddenly had a desire to become a pastry chef. Forget investigative work…pastries is where it's at.

"What do you two want?" Chef Quinn demanded. "I'm busy here. Are you with the police department?"

"Chef Quinn, may we ask you a couple questions real quick?" Aunt Shirley said, breezing by Chef Quinn's question.

The Chef glared at Aunt Shirley. It was on the tip of my tongue to warn her what could happen to a woman's face if she continued to torque her face that way…but I refrained. Sometimes you have to learn by your own mistakes.

"If it's about what just happened, I'll tell you right now you and your department made a *huge* mistake arresting Chef Benoit!" Chef Quinn snapped.

"What makes you think so?" Aunt Shirley asked.

Chef Quinn looked aghast at Aunt Shirley's question. "What makes me think so? Hello...because he didn't do it! If anyone did it, it's that two-timing hussy, Maureen."

"Why Maureen?" I asked.

I heard another squeak from the young assistant pastry chef. She ducked her head and all but fled full speed from us, the pastry cart nearly toppling the fabulous desserts.

My heart nearly pitched right along with the desserts. I narrowed my eyes at the girl. She'd better not do anything harmful to those desserts, because within the hour, those desserts were going in my stomach.

Every single one of them.

Chef Quinn reached over and started cutting another apple tart without looking at us. Her teeth were so tightly clutched, she had to pry them apart to speak.

"Why Maureen? I'll tell you why. She's a hussy, that's why. Flaunting herself around this kitchen like she's someone." Chef Quinn snorted. "She's a glorified waitress. That's all she is!"

"I heard she was seeing Chef Benoit," I said challengingly. A part of me wanted to put this snarky woman in her place.

Chef Quinn scoffed. "He was just humoring her. There's no *way* he actually cares for her. She was just a small dalliance. He deserves someone better. Someone more his class. Someone..." Chef Quinn trailed off and shot Maureen another glare across the expansive kitchen.

"Someone like you?" I asked softly. I'd seen this kind of narcissistic crazy before.

Chef Quinn's eyes snapped back at me and she curled her upper lip. "Exactly! I'm at least a chef like he is. Instead, Chef Benoit has taken to slumming."

Chef Quinn obviously needed to cut back on the meds. Or maybe increase them...I wasn't sure.

Luckily this would have no bearing on how yummy her desserts were. Didn't they say the more over-the-top the chef, the better the creation? If so, I had no doubt her desserts were going to explode with deliciousness in my mouth.

"Why would Maureen and Chef Benoit dating have any bearing on why Philippe Bernard was killed?" Aunt Shirley asked.

Mind off the dessert, Sinclair! Pay attention!

Chef Quinn slammed down the knife she was using to cut the tart. "I'll tell you why. Because suddenly Bernard was all over Maureen. Talking with her privately in his office. Whispering in her ear and making her laugh. They were rubbing their relationship right under Chef Benoit's nose!"

More reason for Chef Benoit to kill Philippe Bernard, not Maureen.

"Then Wednesday night before Philippe was killed, Maureen made this big announcement to her servers she's thinking of quitting. Doing something different with her life."

Funny Maureen hadn't mentioned that little fact when we spoke Wednesday night.

Aunt Shirley's brow furrowed. "Again, I see no reason for Maureen to kill Philippe just because she might get a different job."

Chef Quinn snorted.

I still had to call her on her ridiculousness. "You think Philippe called it off that fast, so Maureen sneaked into his office, pulled out a knife, and slashed him?"

Chef Quinn shrugged. "Sounds good to me. Or maybe they got into a big fight when she told him she was leaving and she stabbed him in anger. Either scenario works for me."

But it doesn't for me.

"Has Maureen mentioned leaving since Wednesday night?" I asked. "Did she say anything tonight?"

"Heavens no. Why would she? One lover is dead, the other hauled away for a crime *she* committed. She'll ride her wave of glory here until the police come to their senses and finally haul her in for the murder."

64

Something told me that was just wishful thinking from an angry, jealous, bitter woman.

"Can I ask you something?" I said, unable to hide the disgust in my voice. "Is that what you honestly believe? That Maureen killed Philippe Bernard because he possibly broke up with her and she couldn't date *both* men?"

"I wouldn't put anything past a woman who has been scorned and is angry."

Truer words, my dear. Truer words!

I rolled my eyes at Aunt Shirley. I really didn't think Chef Quinn had anything more relevant to tell us, and I really wanted a drink.

We thanked her and hurried back to the double doors. The kitchen was in full swing by now, and I just prayed we'd get out without getting caught. I pushed the doors open and stopped in my tracks.

"What're you both doing back here?" Holly Barrow demanded when she saw Aunt Shirley and me. "You aren't allowed back here."

"My aunt got turned around," I said quickly. "She's had a little too much to drink, and I came back to find her."

"Yes. My 'polgies," Aunt Shirley slurred, weaving back and forth on her heels. "Seems I had a wee too much to drink and I got turnt round."

Aunt Shirley stumbled into Holly, and I couldn't help but snicker. Aunt Shirley's pretend drunk always worked. No one wanted to call out an old woman for drinking too much.

"Oh, well," Holly hedged. "I guess I can see that happening. But please go back to your seats now."

"I have her," I promised. "We were just leaving."

"Yup," Aunt Shirley giggled. "Just leavin' this place."

I grabbed Aunt Shirley by the arm and hauled butt from the kitchen area. Weaving our way in and out of the crowded tables, I realized we'd been in the kitchen long enough for the restaurant to fill up. Luckily our food hadn't arrived yet.

"I was beginning to get worried," Mom sighed as we fell into our chairs, snickering.

"What's so funny?" Paige asked. "What did you two do?"

I told them how Aunt Shirley did her pretend drunk stunt and how Holly didn't know how to take it.

"Well, you're in luck," Mindy quipped, "because we got you both another drink just in case you needed it after your adventure."

I grinned and grabbed the full French Kiss in front of me. I loved my family and friends. They knew just what I needed all the time.

"So tell us," Paige said. "What did you learn?"

It was on the tip of my tongue to tell her we learned nothing. That the chef we talked to was bitter and angry...but I suddenly realized she did tell us one bit of news. "Maureen told her servers Wednesday night before the murder that she planned on quitting."

Aunt Shirley grinned at me. "Nice work. I wondered if you'd pick up on that."

We fist bumped and grinned like idiots at each other.

"Why is that important?" Mindy asked as she took a sip of her cocktail.

"Because," I said, "she gave us the impression Wednesday night that she wasn't sure she was ready to quit her job and go to management school."

"Your dinner is ready," Maureen announced as she and another server sidled up to the table, their arms loaded with dishes.

Everyone oohed and aahed over the plates as they were set in front of us. The spices from my boeuf bourguignon wafted up to me, and my mouth started to salivate. I swiped my pinky in the dark, brown sauce and took a quick lick. I couldn't suppress the moan as it rang from deep in my throat.

"That good?" Mom teased.

"You have no idea!"

66

"There you are," Maureen said as she placed my wine in front of me.

I was glad she remembered. Even though I still had a partially full French Kiss left, I didn't think it would taste very good with the beef. Of course, I'm no fool...the French Kiss would taste magnificent with the desserts I planned on gorging on later.

"Anything else I can get you ladies?" Maureen asked.

"Do you like your job here?" I asked.

My question obviously took her by surprise. "Yes. I enjoy my job here immensely. Short of what's happened the last couple days, of course." Her eyes suddenly sparkled. "Why? Are you thinking about applying?"

I chuckled because I knew that's what I was supposed to do. But my mind was busy trying to figure out why she would tell us she wasn't sure she wanted to leave her job and attend management school, yet tell the servers she was ready to quit.

The five of us immersed ourselves in the flavors and textures of our meal—stealing from each other's plates. My favorite was Aunt Shirley's meal. She'd decided on the sea bass, and the minute I put the fish on my tongue, I almost wished I'd ordered it instead. The buttery richness of the fish popped and melted on my tongue.

We decided to share desserts, too. We had a couple chocolate Eclairs, a crème brûlée, and a lemon soufflé. All three were just fine paired with my French Kiss.

"How was everything?" Maureen asked as she placed the bill in front of us.

I groaned and rubbed my stomach. "It was amazing. Just as good as Wednesday night."

Maureen let out a sigh of relief. "Good to know. I mean, not that I didn't think Chef Keller could run the kitchen on his own...it's just nice to hear he did well."

"That's right," I said. "With Chef Benoit's arrest tonight, Chef Keller is now running the kitchen."

And just how far would he go to run the kitchen?

"I'm sure Chef Benoit will be back tomorrow," Maureen said with forced assurance. "And he'll be so happy to know that the years of training Chef Keller paid off. He stepped up just fine in his shoes."

I bit my lip, unsure of how to ask the next question. "Maureen, do you think Aunt Shirley and I could talk with Chef Keller after he gets off tonight?"

Maureen reached up and rubbed her temple. "Why?"

"I just need to ask him a couple questions," I prodded. "I promise I won't take up but five minutes of his time."

"Hold on."

Maureen marched stiffly away, her back ramrod straight. "She doesn't look happy," Paige said.

"If she wants this case solved," Aunt Shirley said, "she won't stand in the way."

Maureen marched back to our table a few minutes later. "He says he'll give you five minutes. After that he's leaving."

"Done," I said quickly. "We'll stop by around eleven to speak with him."

By the time we paid our bill and left for the magic show, I was stuffed and just a little tipsy. What in the world possessed Aunt Shirley to buy tickets to a magic and illusion show I'll never know.

The line to get into the theater was packed. Luckily for Aunt Shirley, there were slots close by she could play while Mom, Paige, Mindy, and I kept her spot. From the thumbs up signs and small jigs, I figured she was either winning big or pretending she was. With Aunt Shirley you never knew what was the truth and what was a lie. It's what made her so good as a private investigator. She once told me people will believe anything you say if you say it with confidence.

The small marquee sign above the entrance to the theater announcing Harry Blackbourn Magic was so bright I almost wished for sunglasses.

68

"This is definitely bizarre pre-party bachelorette entertainment," Paige said as she laid her head on my shoulder, "even by Aunt Shirley's standards."

I laughed, bumping into her huge stomach. "How are you and the babies holding up?"

"We're tired. I just hope the seats aren't made for skinny people. I don't think I can do a couple hours on a hard, flat surface with the babies fighting for space."

"Anytime you want to go back up to the room," Mom said sympathetically, "you can. No one would fault you."

"I'm sure I'll be okay. At least I won't have to worry about getting dragged up on stage." Paige pointed to a poster on the wall advertising a larger-than-life Harry Blackbourn performing a trick using his overly teased and hairsprayed blonde assistant inside the see-through glass container. "I'm so big I won't fit in the box."

I chuckled at her remark. I hated to say it, but she was probably right. I leaned forward and tried to get a better look at the poster. For some reason, the blonde woman seemed familiar to me.

Totally impossible, I concluded. I didn't know a single person in Las Vegas. But, still, I couldn't help but think I'd seen her somewhere.

Before I could ponder too much on it, the line started to move. I ran over to get Aunt Shirley and haul her back in line. She cashed out, grabbed her voucher from the slot machine, and handed it to me. "In case you feel lucky at some point this weekend."

I glanced down and noticed she'd won twenty-five dollars. I laughed. "Only you can win twenty-five dollars in fifteen minutes."

"When are you gonna learn I'm all that and a bag of chips?" Aunt Shirley quipped as she threaded her arms through mine.

I grinned wickedly at her. "Old Man Jenkins tells me that about you all the time."

Aunt Shirley's face turned red. "Pshaw! That old fool! He wouldn't know what to do with me if he caught me."

I wasn't so sure of that. I'd never seen a man so in love in all my life. I was just waiting for the day Old Man Jenkins finally caught Aunt Shirley. I was sure neither one of them would be prepared for the sparks that would fly.

CHAPTER 10

"That was amazing," I said as we slowly made our way out of the theater after the show. "I was honestly blown away by all the magic and illusions."

"It *was* good," Paige agreed. "And can I just say…I loved the assistant's pixie haircut and color."

My eye caught the poster advertising the magic show and I frowned, suddenly understanding why I was so thrown by the assistant. The poster advertised a long-haired curly blonde being captured in the glass container, while the assistant in the show tonight had been a short-haired dark girl with a pixie-like cut. Even their body types were different. Tonight's girl had been more angular and thin.

"I think it's time they updated their poster, though," I said as I pointed to the framed picture on the wall.

Aunt Shirley snapped her finger. "That's it! I knew something was bothering me. I just couldn't put my finger on it."

The whole group stopped and stared open-mouthed at me. I looked behind me, certain I was missing out on something.

I saw nothing.

"What?" I asked.

Paige continued to stare at me with wide eyes and mouth hung open. I turned to Mom and Mindy…they had the same astonished look.

Aunt Shirley slung an arm around my shoulder and gave me a squeeze. "I'm so proud of you! They're just in shock is all."

"Why?" I asked again. I could hear the pride in Aunt Shirley's voice. I knew I'd missed something, but I didn't know what.

"You figured out a clue before I did," Aunt Shirley said matter-of-factly. "All night I kept murmuring to your mom that something was off. And she kept telling me it was magic, it was supposed to be off. Put that feeling kept coming back to me. I just couldn't put my finger on it. And you solved the mystery. I couldn't be prouder!"

I scoffed at their reaction to me. "It was just a simple observation."

Aunt Shirley smiled knowingly at me and then Mom. "It was more than that. You don't give yourself enough credit."

"What's on your agenda now?" Mindy asked, breaking the awkward silence that had fallen over us.

I smiled at her, thankful for her attempt. It was no surprise how Mom and Paige felt about my continued involvement with Aunt Shirley and her murder-solving antics.

"I think right now," Aunt Shirley announced, "I'm going to go show Ryli how to play craps tonight. Any takers?"

I knew she said the last part to ward off any real takers. That's how Aunt Shirley worked her magic. She took the offensive instead of defensive. There wasn't a single person standing in front of us that wanted to tag along and watch Aunt Shirley teach me craps. They knew it was bound to get out of hand.

Paige shook her head. "Something tells me you two will be down here all night. Me and the babies are calling it a night. I need to soak my feet and catch a few minutes of sleep." She rubbed her hands lovingly over her belly. "I'm so exhausted, but I know this feeling is nothing like what I'm going to be going through when the babies actually arrive. I'll never get a good night's sleep!"

Mom chuckled. "Trust me, you will. Your mom and I will make sure you and the babies are taken care of as much as possible."

Tears fell from Paige's eyes and she wiped them away. "I'm so emotional lately. But thank you, Janine. Having family around helps so much. I know you guys won't leave me hanging high and dry. It's just my nerves talking."

Mom gave Paige a squeeze. "Everything will be amazing, just you wait."

"I was hoping to do a little more shopping in the boutiques," Mindy said. "I promised Hank I wouldn't buy anything…which means I need to buy something soon!"

We all laughed at her mischievous announcement. Rarely did Mindy buck Hank, but when she did, she did it with flare.

Mom bit her lip. "I'll go back upstairs with you, Paige, if you'd like."

Paige patted Mom's shoulder. "Go shopping with Mindy. I'll be fine."

Mom grinned. "Was it that obvious?"

"Yes!" we all exclaimed.

Mom shrugged sheepishly.

We parted ways—Mom and Mindy headed to the shopping area of the hotel, Paige waddled off to the elevator, and Aunt Shirley and I strolled to the perfect craps table.

The one where Arthur Tisdale was currently stationed.

The ladies had already informed Aunt Shirley and me of Arthur's nightly schedule and that he kept his electronic key in his front pocket. Usually he'd take a woman out to dinner, and afterward there would be gambling at the craps table. Tonight, Arthur Tisdale was alone—no new mark or unsuspecting female for him to dupe. A plus for us.

We wedged in between Arthur and another middle-aged cowboy in a ten-gallon felt hat. Aunt Shirley thrust her hands in her purse and whipped out three one hundred dollar bills and threw them down on the table. No surprise, this immediately caught the eye of Arthur.

"Hello there, lovely lady." He bowed stiffly, his portly belly falling below his belt.

Aunt Shirley batted her lashes. Hand to God, she batted her lashes! "Hello there, handsome. My name's Shirley, what's yours?"

Arthur sucked in his belly and thrust out his concave chest. "Names Arthur. Arthur Tisdale. And might I say it's a pleasure to meet you Miss Shirley. It is Miss, right?"

Watching Aunt Shirley flirt with Old Man Jenkins was a hoot. This felt sinister and downright dirty. Of course, it's probably because I love Old Man Jenkins…and this man was definitely *not* Old Man Jenkins.

"It's Miss. I ain't never been married," Aunt Shirley boasted. "And this is my niece, Ryli."

I stuck my hand out to shake his, but Arthur didn't even look at me. I can't say I was too disappointed.

Aunt Shirley turned back to the table. "Excuse me, Arthur. I'm going to play a couple hands if you don't mind."

"Not at all. Go right ahead."

I snorted at the thought that this man felt the need to give Aunt Shirley permission to place a bet. He had no idea the barracuda he was tangling with.

"Let's do a hundred behind the four and a hundred behind the ten," Aunt Shirley said as she flopped the chips down on the table, along with her little buy-in bet.

My eyes popped open. That was quite a chunk of change Aunt Shirley was throwing down just to snag the guy's attention. It would be one thing if she won, but I'd never known Aunt Shirley to gamble before. Did she even know what she was doing? I'd never even seen a craps table before.

Arthur's beady little eyes raked over Aunt Shirley. "Very nice. Nothing sexier than a lady who knows how to play and win."

Gag!

74

Aunt Shirley preened and let out a tiny giggle. I almost hit the floor. It always gave me the willies when Aunt Shirley did her flirtatious giggle. Usually she had deep belly laughs that matched her stalwart personality. To hear such a delicate sound come from her was nearly my undoing. I had to literally bite my lip to keep from snickering.

Aunt Shirley batted her eyes at the portly, thick-chested man. His dark eyes shot up in surprise and a very subtle predatory look came over his face.

There's the hook!

"I've been playing for a few years now," Aunt Shirley admitted. "Not that I'm telling you my age."

Another giggle.

Arthur lifted a meaty hand in the air. A scantily-clad waitress scurried over. He stared intently at Aunt Shirley. "Two rum and sodas."

He never even bothered to glance my way to see if I wanted anything. When the waitress looked expectantly at me, I asked for a water.

"Trying to get me drunk and take advantage of me?" Aunt Shirley laughed.

"Maybe," the elderly man smirked. "Are you looking to get taken advantaged of?"

There's the line!

"You think you're man enough to handle me?" Aunt Shirley purred as she turned back to focus on the table.

"I think I'm definitely man enough to handle you," Arthur said, his eyes never leaving Aunt Shirley's stash of chips.

"Do you know what you're doing?" I hissed as the guy running the show shoved a pair of dice to a gentleman down at the far end of the table.

Aunt Shirley chuckled. "Yes. Encourage him to roll a seven."

I watched in what seemed like slow motion as the guy tossed the dice onto the velvet-topped surface. The dice continued to tumble for a few more seconds before coming to a stop in front of me.

"Seven!" the guy in charge yelled.

I let out a scream. I didn't exactly know what it meant, but Aunt Shirley said that was the number we wanted.

The man gave Aunt Shirley a couple chips. "Take it down or leave it up?"

Aunt Shirley smiled at me before saying, "Leave it up. I think we have one more roll in us."

I rolled my eyes. Leave it to Aunt Shirley to push the boundaries. I watched as the guy at the end of the table picked up the dice.

"What number now?" I hissed.

"Same. Seven."

I closed my eyes and chanted the number seven over and over.

"Seven!"

I screamed and jumped up and down, grasping on to Aunt Shirley for dear life. I didn't care if we'd only won four bucks, I couldn't be more excited.

Aunt Shirley turned to Arthur. "My niece is having a bachelorette party tomorrow night, but I'm free beforehand…say around seven? You wanna play with me?"

Arthur Tisdale barked out a laugh. "More than you know!"

And sinker!

Arthur Tisdale, con man extraordinaire, had just been conned by my Aunt Shirley! Hook…line…and sinker!

"Your drinks," the waitress said as she handed Arthur and Aunt Shirley their glasses. When Arthur made no move to pay for my water or tip the waitress, I quickly dug out a couple dollars from my clutch. She smiled and thanked me. But not before I saw the look of disgust she shot Arthur.

"Take it down or leave it up?" the head guy yelled over again.

"Take it down, please." Aunt Shirley reached over and collected her chips, then tossed them in her purse before picking back up her drink.

It was the perfect distraction. I unscrewed my water bottle and stumbled forward, bumping into Aunt Shirley. On cue, we both pitched our drinks at Arthur Tisdale's lower torso and crotch.

Priceless!

The man stumbled back as though he'd been attacked with a knife instead of water and soda. "You clumsy fool!" he shouted at me. "Look what you did!"

Aunt Shirley and I both leaned over and started frantically brushing the liquid away. Our hands roaming over and then *in* his pockets. He'd barely recovered from the shock of our assault before Aunt Shirley gave me an almost imperceptible nod. She'd gotten his card.

"Oh, Mr. Tisdale," I gushed. "I'm so sorry. Are you okay?"

The short, angry man focused his malevolent gaze on me, giving Aunt Shirley enough time to stick the electronic key card down her bra.

I bit back a short chuckle at the sight. Aunt Shirley never ceased to amuse me at the most inopportune time.

"Now Arthur," Aunt Shirley cooed. "It was just an accident. My niece didn't mean any harm at all."

Not!

"Yes," I said in a robotic tone, "I'm so sorry, Mr. Tisdale."

I did my best to look contrite, but I knew I wasn't pulling it off. Everything about this man disgusted me. And at this point, I didn't care if he knew it or not.

Aunt Shirley leaned into the odious man and flirted some more while I quickly scooped up Aunt Shirley's purse. I was ready to be out of his foul presence.

"We're still on for tomorrow evening, right?" Aunt Shirley said breathlessly, as though she wanted nothing more than to be around him.

Arthur Tisdale hunched his shoulders and tapped his foot. I knew that look. So did Aunt Shirley.

"Here," she said as she thrust a chip at him. "Take this and get your pants dry cleaned."

Can you dry clean seersucker fabric?

The gluttonous gleam in Arthur's eye turned my heart cold. I watched in horror as he snatched the coin out of Aunt Shirley's hand. Now, more than ever, I knew this man was evil through and through.

"Thanks," Arthur mumbled as he tossed the coin in the air and caught it. "How about I pick you up at your room around seven. What's your room number?"

My pulse stuttered. No way did I want this lecherous man to know where we were staying.

"Like I said," Aunt Shirley said smoothly, "it's Ryli's bachelorette party tomorrow night. We'll probably already be out. How about I meet you at Ooh La La, the French Café out by the boutique stores?"

Arthur raked his eyes once more down Aunt Shirley's body, as though sizing her up. I barely contained the bile that rose in my throat.

"Fine," Arthur spat. "I'll meet you there."

He cast one more appreciative glance at Aunt Shirley's purse I had folded in my arms before turning back to the table dismissing us.

"Whew!" Aunt Shirley exclaimed as we hurried away. "That man is so vile. I feel like I need to go upstairs and shower!"

I snorted. "Truer words."

Aunt Shirley looked at her watch. "I need to sit down. We still have almost an hour before we're to be at the restaurant to question Chef Keller. Let's go upstairs for a while."

We rushed to the elevator, ignoring the shrieks, whistles, and overall hustle and bustle still playing out around us. I punched the up arrow and waited impatiently for the elevator doors to open.

We stepped inside and both of us exhaled a sigh of relief. Arthur Tisdale was one unsavory dude.

"It scares me how efficient we've become," Aunt Shirley said as she yanked Arthur Tisdale's electronic key card out of her bra.

I didn't say anything…just silently lifted a clutched fist in the air. Aunt Shirley gave me a fist bump.

"Word," I said.

CHAPTER 11

"Psst. Aunt Shirley. You need to wake up. It's almost eleven o'clock."

Aunt Shirley smacked her lips. An appalling sight considering her false teeth had fallen out of her mouth while she'd been resting her eyes.

She reached down and shoved the false teeth back in. "I must have dozed off for a minute."

I shuddered at the sight, but forged ahead. "It's almost eleven. We need to head downstairs to the restaurant."

In truth, I really just wanted to crawl into bed and go to sleep. Let Detective Dickerson solve the case. But I knew Aunt Shirley would have my hide if I let her sleep through the night.

"Give me a minute to go to the bathroom," Aunt Shirley said as she hoisted herself off the couch. "My bladder ain't what it used to be."

A few minutes later she was ready to go, teeth firmly latched in place and bladder empty.

We crept out of our suite and rode the elevator to the casino floor. When the doors opened, bells and whistles and excited voices greeted us. I guess it didn't matter if it was eleven in the morning or eleven at night…casino sounds were all the same. How in the world these people stayed up so late was news to me.

We veered off from the gambling area and made our way to the entertainment and food service area to the exquisite French restaurant. Only a handful of lights were on and the sign read CLOSED.

I knocked on the door and the same maître d that had seated us previously answered. He frowned when he saw us. "We're closed. You'll have to come back tomorrow."

"Maureen said it was okay if we came by," I said.

"Well, Maureen doesn't make the rules. Holly is now the manager, so I'll have to get permission from her."

Without another word, the snooty man turned on his heel and walked away…shutting the door in our faces.

"I'm thinking he needs a nap," Aunt Shirley said.

I laughed. "I think *I* need a nap."

The door was quickly opened and Holly Barrows stood in the doorway. She definitely looked more relaxed since the first night I saw her.

"May I help you?" she asked snootily.

"I don't know if you remember us," I said, "but we were here Wednesday night, the night of Philippe's murder. And again tonight."

A wary look came over Holly's face as she looked at Aunt Shirley. "Yes. I've seen you in here many times."

I tried to put her at ease. "And I've seen you. You're doing a great job through these difficult times. The way you've stepped up to the plate to do your part in this tragedy is admirable."

Holly's cheeks turned pink and behind her enormous glasses tears filled her eyes. "Thank you. I'm trying really hard. I've only been here six months, so Philippe was still training me. I just hope I'm doing him proud."

I put my hand on her arm. "You are. Trust me, this place is running smoothly considering the horror just experienced."

Holly tucked a strand of her flowing hair behind her ear. "What can I do for you?"

I was about to tell her that Maureen said we could talk to Chef Keller, but Aunt Shirley cut me off.

"As my niece said, we've been in here two nights now. And not only have *you* been making the transition smooth in this tragedy, but so has Chef Keller. Our meals have been divine each night. Earlier, we'd asked Maureen if we could stop by and give our praises to the Chef when everything had quieted down."

Holly bit down on her lower lip. "Well, that's a little unusual. But I guess since you guys have been in here both nights and can judge for yourselves how smoothly the transition has been, I guess I can allow it."

She stepped back and invited us in. "I think Chef is still in the kitchen finalizing tomorrow's menu. The only thing I ask is that you make it quick, please."

"You got it," I said.

We followed her to the back of the restaurant, through the swinging doors, and into the quiet kitchen. A huge change from just a few hours ago.

Maureen saw us and her eyes widened. She excused herself from the two other servers she was talking with and walked over to where we were. "I'm so sorry! I forgot you were coming by tonight." She looked warily at Holly. "I told them they could—"

Holly cut her off. "It's okay. I'm aware of why they're here. I told them to make it quick."

Maureen bit her lip. "So it's okay with you if they talk to Chef Keller?"

Holly frowned. "Why wouldn't it be?"

Maureen shrugged and walked back over to the other servers cleaning up the station.

I almost felt bad duping the two women. Poor Maureen had no idea we'd lied to Holly and said we wanted to compliment Chef Keller instead of drill him on what he knew about the murder. But if we played our cards right, Holly would never have to know.

"Chef Keller," Holly said loudly. "These two women would like to compliment you on the dinner you served them tonight. I told them it would be okay to speak with you for just a few minutes."

Chef Keller didn't even bother to look up. "I'm a little busy."

"Chef Keller, I'd really appreciate it if you took a few minutes to speak with these two ladies." Holly's voice took on a don't-mess-with-me-I'm-the-boss-now tone.

Chef Keller looked up and scowled. "Fine. Three minutes."

Holly nodded curtly and walked away.

I hadn't felt this awkward in a long time. Chef Keller's hat was gone, his blonde hair sticking to his scalp. His chiseled features hadn't relaxed one bit. His mouth was set in a flat line, and his eyes were hard and angry.

I cleared my throat and began. "Chef Keller, my name is Ryli, and this is Aunt Shirley. We've been eating here for the past—well, basically for the past two nights you've been open. Our first night, Wednesday, Chef Benoit was in charge, and since then you have taken over. We just first wanted to say the meals have always been delicious. My aunt and I couldn't tell a difference in chefs from Wednesday night to tonight."

Chef Keller lifted one brow. "Of course you wouldn't be able to tell a difference. I've been training under Chef Benoit for years. On any given night, I am ready to step into his shoes."

He bent over a piece of paper and started writing again, obviously dismissing us.

"I guess it's lucky for you then that you finally had the opportunity," Aunt Shirley's hard voice matched his.

Chef Keller looked up and smiled. The smile didn't reach his eyes. "Meaning?"

I heard the threat behind the question.

Aunt Shirley shrugged. "Meaning I guess it's fortuitous for you that you finally got the chance to step up and prove you can cook."

Chef Keller's nostrils flared. "Madam, not only did I study at *the* most famous culinary school in France, but I have also studied under many famous master chefs. More famous than Chef Benoit." He all but spat Benoit's name. "Of course I would be ready to step in at a moment's notice and run the kitchen."

"My aunt was just trying to say that you've done a great job filling in."

His cold eyes flickered over me. "It didn't sound like that to me."

"Okay then," Aunt Shirley said. "Let's just put the cards on the table. Did you kill Philippe Bernard because he wouldn't give you the chance to be a master chef? You obviously have the training, have studied under more famous chefs, and by your tone you don't like Chef Benoit."

Chef Keller scowled at Aunt Shirley. "Let me make this perfectly clear...I have no problem with Chef Benoit. He's a great chef. I know in order to be a master chef in charge of my own kitchen, I will probably have to leave this position. I am still here. Hence, I don't feel the need to get rid of the competition as you seem to think I do." He leaned in closer to us. "I also had no problem with Philippe Bernard. Not everyone in this kitchen could say that."

"I've heard Chef Benoit and Philippe argued quite a bit," Aunt Shirley said.

Chef Keller scoffed. "They were always at each other's throats. That's typical of a head chef and a manager. It's almost expected." He paused, then added," But, the night Philippe was murdered, those two *had* been going at it all night. It wasn't just the typical head chef and manager bickering, there was something more to it than that. We all felt it."

"Do you know why?" I asked.

Chef Keller didn't say anything for a long time. Just when I thought he wasn't going to answer, he looked over in Maureen's direction and snickered. "Let's just say I think it's because Chef Benoit has had his eye on a tasty little morsel here at the restaurant and didn't appreciate Philippe honing in."

I gasped. "Did you seriously just call Maureen a tasty little morsel? That's creepy and sexist."

Chef Keller shrugged indifferently, as though Maureen wasn't even worth a dignified answer.

Aunt Shirley ignored my outburst. "Are you implying that Chef Benoit did indeed kill Philippe?"

Chef Keller shrugged again, as though he didn't care one way or the other. "I'll tell you the same thing I told that other detective I've spoken with a couple times...Chef Benoit took a break at one point in the evening, something he normally does not do. I have no idea where he went or what he did on that break."

"He simply could have gone to the restroom," I argued.

"And he simply could have gone to Philippe's office and killed him," Chef Keller argued back. "Now, if you'll excuse me, I need to get back to tomorrow's menu. As you said, with Chef Benoit out of the picture, this is my time to shine. I plan on taking full advantage."

"Did you take a break Wednesday night?" I asked.

Chef Keller narrowed his eyes at me. "Yes. Once Chef Benoit returned and everything was stable in the kitchen, I did take a small break."

"One more question," Aunt Shirley said. "Did you know about the announcement Maureen had made earlier in the evening before Philippe was murdered about quitting the restaurant?"

Chef Keller rolled his eyes and clicked his pen rapidly. "Not that I lower myself to gossip amongst the wait staff, but I may have gotten word about Maureen's sudden announcement right at the start of the dinner rush."

"Do you know why she planned on quitting?" I asked.

Chef Keller leveled his eyes on me. "No, I do not. Like I said, I don't make it a point to mingle with the staff. Now, please leave so I can get back to work."

"C'mon," Aunt Shirley said as she dragged me out of the arrogant man's presence.

I was suddenly bone tired. Sometimes dealing with the most unsavory of characters will do that to me.

"I can't tell if Chef Keller is pointing his finger at Maureen or Chef Benoit," I said as we headed back through the kitchen's double doors. "He seemed to be all over the place."

"I agree. One minute he's throwing suspicion Maureen's way, the next minute, it's Chef Benoit doing the killing."

I spotted Maureen still talking with her friend. "I also want to know why Maureen suddenly announced she was quitting earlier that night, and yet she said nothing to us. And I want to know if she still plans on it."

Aunt Shirley grinned wickedly at me. "Let's go ask."

We veered over to where Maureen was. Both women looked dead on their feet.

"Maureen," I said, "do you think we can ask you a quick question?"

Maureen looked stricken, as though she was afraid of what we might say. I heard her swallow hard.

"Charli, I'll call you tomorrow," Maureen said dismissively.

"Sure thing, Maureen."

The girl gave us a strange look before she picked up her purse and walked out the door. Once she was gone, I turned to a shaken Maureen.

"Have you heard anything more regarding Chef Benoit?" I asked, hoping to put her at ease.

Maureen shook her head. "I just checked my cell phone and still no call."

"I'm sure you'll hear something soon, dear," Aunt Shirley said.

I nodded encouragingly. "Listen, I just need to know one thing. Aunt Shirley and I have heard something from a couple different people." It amazed me how easily I could lie when I needed to. "We heard that early in the evening before Philippe was murdered that you made an announcement you were quitting your job."

86

"You heard about that?" I could hear the quiver of fear in Maureen's voice.

"Yes. Can you tell me why you were going to quit?" I asked. "And why you didn't tell us about it the night we questioned you in the bathroom?"

"It's really not relevant right now, so I'd rather not say."

I'd rather you did.

I crossed my arms over my chest. "I thought you told us you hadn't made up your mind yet on whether or not you were going to go to management school? Seems to me if you're announcing to everyone you plan on quitting, that you indeed *had* made a decision."

Tears filled Maureen's eyes and she twisted her hands nervously in front of her. "It's not like that. It's something else."

"Something else?" Aunt Shirley probed. "So you don't plan on quitting anymore?"

Maureen caught Holly's eye across the room as Holly slowly made her way over to us.

"No. I don't," Maureen hissed. "I really need this job right now. And I'd appreciate it if you forgot all about it."

"Forgot about what?" Holly asked as she stopped in front of us.

"Nothing," Maureen said quickly. "The ladies were just leaving."

Holly smiled and shook our hands. "We love hearing feedback from our customers. Thank you for taking the time to come in."

Holly ushered Aunt Shirley and me out of the restaurant and into the bright lights of the casino.

"Impressions?" Aunt Shirley asked.

"First and foremost, I think Chef Keller is a vile man."

"Agreed," Aunt Shirley said.

"And secondly, I think there's a lot more to Maureen's story than she's telling. Although, I don't think Maureen and Philippe got into a fight and she killed him in anger. Too many people have commented on the fact Philippe's been doting on her lately. So much so that Philippe and Chef Benoit had been fighting. Then Chef Benoit takes a break, something the Chef normally doesn't do, and a little while later Maureen announced she's quitting her job. Oh, and then a little while after that a body is discovered by Maureen with her fingerprints all over the murder weapon. And now Maureen is telling us she doesn't want to quit. It doesn't make sense."

"I would agree. But I think we're missing something vital here. I don't think it's as black and white as either Chef Benoit killing Philippe or Maureen killing Philippe."

I threw up my hands. "I was afraid of this."

Aunt Shirley smacked her false teeth together in glee. "You heard Chef Keller say he's been dying to step into Chef Benoit's shoes for years. Maybe he decided to finally act. He knows Chef Benoit and Philippe have been arguing lately, he also knows the Chef has excused himself to take a break, and Chef Keller admits to taking a break a few minutes after Chef Benoit returns. Maybe Chef Keller went into Philippe's office and slashed him, thinking everyone else might throw suspicion to Chef Benoit. I mean, Chef Keller did. He drew suspicion away from him and onto Chef Benoit *and* Maureen."

"I suppose you're right." I sighed and looped my arms through hers. "This isn't going to be an easy solve, is it?"

"They never are, dear. They never are. Now, let's go upstairs to bed. My falsies are killing me."

"Yes, I noticed you're having a tough time with your teeth."

Aunt Shirley grinned and hitched up her sagging chest. "Those aren't the falsies I'm talking about."

"Gross!"

"What? I had to make sure Arthur Tisdale looked my way."

"Why would you even bring fake boobs with you on this trip?"

88

Aunt Shirley gathered me close to her side. "I think a better question to ask is why *wouldn't* I bring fake boobs with me to a bachelorette party weekend. Ryli, my precious, men are men no matter how old they get."

We sneaked back into the suite with no one the wiser. I whispered good night to Aunt Shirley and headed for the bedroom. I was glad to see Paige sleeping. She'd tossed and turned last night, trying to find a comfortable position.

I dug my cell phone out of my purse before tossing the clutch onto the chair by the bed. I sent a text to Garrett asking if he was still up. I got an instant reply back.

Tiptoeing into the bathroom for some privacy, I called Garrett.

"Hey, Sin."

I shivered at the timbre in his voice. It always undid me. "Hi. Long night at work?"

"Not too bad. How about you?"

"Same. Not too bad. Had a lot of fun with the girls."

Garrett chuckled. "You're being too aloof. What did you really do tonight?"

I sighed and filled him in…not only with the snatch and grab with Arthur Tisdale, but with the questioning of Chef Keller.

"I somehow feel you're losing the focus of why you're supposed to be in Vegas," Garrett said dryly.

I laughed softly. "You sound like Mom."

"Yes, well, I've always thought your mother was a very smart woman."

"We're being careful, don't worry."

"Really?" Garrett asked. "You don't think Arthur isn't going to wonder where his key went?"

I frowned. "I don't think so. He'll probably think it fell out of his pocket and he lost it at one of the tables. The front desk will just give him a new one."

Garrett was silent for a moment. "So you're gonna try and nab him tomorrow, is that right?"

"Yes. And please don't try and talk me out of it. I'm doing it for these ladies. They've been duped by an odious man and someone needs to stand for them."

Garrett sighed. "I honestly love this altruistic quality about you."

"Thank you."

"But I also feel I need to remind you that's what police are for. Let the professionals handle it."

I bristled a little. "If the police get involved, the rings will probably be taken into evidence. However, if we can catch Arthur red-handed, we can threaten to expose him to the police unless he hands the jewelry over."

"So you are positively set for this to happen tomorrow?"

"Yes. Tomorrow evening. I'll call you when we apprehend him."

"Okay. I love you Ryli Jo."

I smiled into the phone. "And I love you Garrett James."

CHAPTER 12

"That spa package this morning really hit the spot." I sipped happily on my second mimosa and tried to ignore the jealous look Paige was sending my way as she sipped her green tea.

"That *was* a nice surprise, Aunt Shirley," Mom said. "What brought that on?"

Aunt Shirley grinned at me. "Let's just say I had a nice roll of the dice last night."

"You won enough to pay for all of us to be treated to a facial *and* hour-long massage?" Mindy asked as she sat down on the settee next to Mom. "Wow. I should have stayed with you guys and forgone the shopping."

I laughed at took another drink. "You should have seen Aunt Shirley last night. In two rolls, she raked it in!"

Mom frowned. "It doesn't always happen that way. You can lose just as easily as win."

I gave her my best exasperated look. "I know, Mom. But we had to make sure we caught the eye of Arthur Tisdale. And boy did we ever! Aunt Shirley has a date with him tonight."

"This is Saturday! Your bachelorette party is tonight," Mom said. "You two are not doing your mystery thing on your bachelorette party night!"

"Simmer down, Janine," Aunt Shirley said. "The party doesn't start until eight. I'm meeting Arthur at seven."

I watched Mom's lips move silently. Nearly thirty years as her child has taught me she was counting to ten before she spoke. I wisely kept my mouth shut and let her continue counting.

"Aunt Shirley, if you make my daughter late for her big night, so help me—"

Aunt Shirley snorted. "I ain't gonna make her late for nothing…be it the naughty show I got us tickets to, or the party afterward."

"Yeah, Mom. Aunt Shirley wouldn't risk—" I cut myself off and turned to Aunt Shirley. "Wait. What naughty show? No one said anything about a naughty show! I'm not gonna watch a bunch of strippers roll around on a stage tonight!"

Aunt Shirley slapped her knee and guffawed, nearly knocking her mimosa off the table. "It's not that kind of naughty show. Although, if I thought for one minute any of you prissy women would embrace strippers, I'd have ordered some." She turned to me and grinned. "Trust me, you'll like this naughty surprise. There's lots of ropes involved."

My hands flew up to my mouth. "You got tickets to that show they're advertising downstairs! The one where the people are practically naked and twirling around on ropes and big circles?"

Aunt Shirley grinned, picked up her glass, and drank half her mimosa in one gulp. That was Aunt Shirley speak for "you got it!"

I racked my brain to recall what all the poster had touted about the performance. Loosely translated it was something like circles and ropes of forbiddance. And didn't it say something like the audience would be pushed to the limits of their taboos?

What the heck does that mean?

I opened my mouth to give Aunt Shirley what-for, but Paige beat me to the punch.

Or so I thought.

"Aunt Shirley, thanks so much for the prenatal massage this morning," Paige said as she rubbed her stomach. "My back, hips, legs—really everything—feels so much better. I feel so good I could probably keep up with you guys most of the day if I had to."

Well, thanks to Paige, I couldn't now give Aunt Shirley a piece of my mind without sounding rude and ungrateful. I picked a grape up off my plate and crammed it in my mouth. Still not satisfied, I downed the last of my mimosa.

"You're welcome, Paige," Aunt Shirley said. "I'm just disappointed I couldn't get that Brazilian wax I wanted. You never know where this date may lead tonight."

My mouth dropped. "First, that's too disgusting to process this early in the day. And second, Tisdale is a creep!"

Aunt Shirley shrugged. "I got needs."

Mom gasped in horror.

"Me, too. I *need* another drink," I moaned to Mindy our mimosa maker.

"You got it," Mindy said, getting up from the settee with obvious glee at my discomfort.

I looked over at Aunt Shirley's grinning face. "You know what? Better make it two more mimosas."

***

"You know," Aunt Shirley snickered as she led me to the elevator a few hours later, "maybe you shouldn't have had those extra drinks. Where I'm taking you next, those drinks may revolt."

I furrowed my brow. I had no idea what her little cryptic message meant, but I knew Aunt Shirley well enough to know I should be scared. If she was warning me ahead of time, it was gonna be bad.

"Do I even want to know where you are taking me now?" I asked as we stood in the elevator. The fact she'd pushed the up arrow to signal the elevator and now pushed the rooftop button didn't escape my hawk-like eyes.

"I'm taking you to your marriage metaphor," Aunt Shirley said proudly.

"Come again?"

"Your marriage metaphor. You'll understand when we get there."

The elevator doors opened and we stepped out onto the paved rooftop. My gaze drifted immediately to the death-defying ride the hotel boasted. No way was I getting on that thing!

I watched the ride make a slow progression two hundred feet straight up in the air. About twenty people sat in a circle, all facing outward so they could see the city spread out before them. Once the ride reached the top, it stopped with a jerk. A hush fell over the crowd as we all waited with baited breath for what was about to happen next. Without warning, the ride fell two hundred feet straight down. Screams and laughter filled the air. Screams from the people riding, and laughter from the people smart enough to be recording the nightmare from the rooftop level.

"Not gonna happen." I turned to get back on the elevator, but Aunt Shirley was faster. She snatched my arm and yanked me over to where thirty or so people were standing in a line.

"This *is* gonna happen," she insisted. "This is your marriage metaphor."

"What?" I said sarcastically as we planted ourselves behind a tall guy wearing Bermuda shorts, sandals, and t-shirt. He had a comforting hand on the shoulder of a scared boy who looked to be around ten years old. "I need to know that marriage will have its ups and downs? Guess what, Aunt Shirley…I already know that! I don't have to go straight up two hundred feet in the air to find that out."

Aunt Shirley shook her head. "It's more than just ups and downs, Ryli. Like this ride, it can be sickening, and exciting, or even cause you to have heart palpitations. It's so many different things. And this ride is gonna show you that. Marriage also makes you wanna throw up during most of it, so be prepared for that, too. Both during the marriage and probably when you get off this ride. I know what a baby you can be."

The guy in front of us snickered. I could tell he was trying not to pay attention to us, but Aunt Shirley didn't exactly know how to whisper.

"You married?" Aunt Shirley asked him.

"Um…" The guy looked around frantically, as though afraid of how to answer. "Yes. My wife is over there with the cell phone getting ready to capture our stupidity. Her words, not mine."

I chuckled. "Your wife has it right. This is ridiculous."

"Tell this young whippersnapper I'm right about the marriage thing. It may be fun when you first start out, like this ride. You're just sitting there waiting, anticipating what will happen next. Then suddenly something does happen, and now you wanna get off, leave the ride behind. But it's too late. And as you move up the ride, your stomach drops with worry, maybe even regret. When you finally reach the top, maybe that's the birth of your first child, and you're so excited. Then wait two seconds and your world will fall apart as you plummet back to the ground. There's fear, delight, horror, anger, and even gratitude that everyone is safe by the time you reach the bottom. But unlike this ride, marriage isn't just a one-time ride. You're gonna be doing this crazy ride thousands of time."

I stood in stunned silence, tears filling my eyes. Aunt Shirley's words went straight to my heart. I'd never heard her speak so eloquently and moving…ever. How did a woman who'd never been married before know just exactly what to say?

The man in front of us cleared his throat. "She's exactly right." He looked down at his son. "Marriage is all those things, plus more. Before our son came along, we'd had a little girl. She was stillborn. The emotions your aunt just expressed—the anticipated excitement then disappointment, anger, worry—my wife and I felt all at one time just from the death of our little girl. Then two years later the next emotional roller coaster came along, and he has been such a blessing to us." The man squeezed his son's shoulder before smiling at Aunt Shirley and me. "But the ride is definitely worth it. Trust me."

The line started moving and he turned back around, gathering his son close to his side. I swiped at the tears that had fallen from my eyes and rolled down my cheeks.

The attendant gave me a smile as I made my way to an empty seat. Aunt Shirley plopped down next to me, giddy with excitement. Me, not so much. Once again I fought down the urge to hurl.

"Watch your head." A young man in a light-blue work uniform reached up and pulled the bar down over me, giving it a couple good jerks for measure.

As he turned to take care of Aunt Shirley, I continued where he left off—pushing up against the metal bar. I'm sure he knew how to do his job, but at minimum wage, I was willing to put a little bit higher price on my life than a couple bucks an hour.

"You sure your heart is strong enough for this ride?" the young man asked.

Aunt Shirley scowled at the boy. "My ticker is just fine, young man. Pull this bar down and stand back!"

"Your funeral lady," the boy muttered as he did what Aunt Shirley demanded.

As the ride made a loud noise and started its slow progression upward, I continued pushing on the bar—just in case. Just in case of what, I don't know. It's not like they could stop the ride going down if the bar suddenly flew off.

"Stop it," Aunt Shirley commanded. "You're missing out on the view."

I stopped pushing on the bar and looked at the scene around me. I could see all of Las Vegas. Heck, I could see what looked like hundreds of miles past Vegas. The people on the streets looked like tiny ants scurrying around. I could hear the clacking of the metal the higher we climbed. Clamping down on the urge to vomit, I closed my eyes and laid my head back on the seat.

Do not vomit! Do not vomit!

"Whooowheee! Isn't this the life, Ryli?"

Aunt Shirley was grinning like a fool, and I suddenly wanted to push her out of the ride and watch her fall as I laughed.

Wow. You need to get a grip, Ryli.

"Like I said," Aunt Shirley continued, "this is like a marriage. You are feeling—"

"How about you not tell me how I'm feeling and just let me ride the rest of this out in peace. Just keep your mouth closed and leave me alone."

Aunt Shirley huffed. "Well, you don't have to take your crappy marriage out on me. My marriage is going great! My man and I are having the time of our lives watching all the people go by. My man and I—"

I blocked out her insane rattling and concentrated on counting the number of clicks the machine made as we went higher and higher in the air. A few minutes later, I was jerked nearly out of my seat. My eyes flew open. The ride had stopped. We were at the top...the whole world was splayed out in front of me in a beautiful display. Unfortunately, it wasn't a display I could appreciate.

"Here we go!" Aunt Shirley cried right before I passed out.

Or at least I assumed I passed out. I really don't remember the rapid descent at all. Next thing I know, we're back on the ground and Aunt Shirley gave me a good shove, yelling about the fantastic catch she'd made.

"What catch?" I mumbled through shivering lips.

"My false teeth practically flew out of my mouth! But don't worry, I was able to get my hands up and shove them back in."

Oh, praises. God knows we wouldn't want you losing your fake teeth. Now, where did the last thirty seconds of my life go you heartless woman!

"Did you enjoy the ride?" the young attendant asked me as I shakily undid my lap belt and he lifted the bar up over my head. I couldn't formulate a response...my teeth were chattering too hard.

"Loved it!" Aunt Shirley exclaimed. "We might need to do this again before we leave."

No, we don't.

"C'mon," Aunt Shirley said as she pulled me out of the enclosed gate of the ride. "I'm in the mood for a mango margarita."

The world tilted and I stumbled over to an area clear of people. Leaning over, I lost a little of my brunch. I heard a couple people shriek and knew they were watching me. But I didn't care. All I wanted was for the world to go back to how it was before I walked out onto the rooftop.

"Yep," Aunt Shirley said dispassionately as she walked over to where I was still bent over, "you've just completed the whole marriage metaphor. You've got vomit everywhere."

By the time an attendant came over and gave me a tissue, and I made my way back to the elevator, I was ready to throttle Aunt Shirley. This had to be the most ridiculous and humiliating thing we'd ever done.

Well, one of the most ridiculous and humiliating. We *had* done some pretty insane things over the year.

"That's me," Aunt Shirley suddenly announced as she whipped out her cell phone from her bra and opened up her text message.

I pressed a hand to my stomach. Even the elevator ride down was making me queasy.

"It's a text from Cheryl Owens," Aunt Shirley said. "Seems Arthur is down in the game room doing some gambling. The girls thought we might want to do some snooping."

I groaned. "I don't think I'm up to it."

"Nonsense! It's the perfect time."

I wasn't the least bit shocked she'd brushed off my protest.

CHAPTER 13

"Nice and slow now," Aunt Shirley whispered as we got off the elevator and made our way to Arthur's room. As of two minutes ago, Arthur was still downstairs gambling. The ladies promised to give us updates every few minutes of his whereabouts.

Aunt Shirley pulled the electronic key card she lifted from Arthur last night and slid it in the slot. "Let's see if Arthur just went to the front desk and asked for another card last night."

The green light popped on.

"Eureka!" Aunt Shirley shouted.

"Shhh. We're supposed to be inconspicuous."

I looked over my shoulder to make sure no one was coming down the hallway from either side.

Aunt Shirley pushed the door open and we rushed in. I let the door fall back softly so we didn't bring attention to ourselves in the room.

Arthur was in a standard-sized room...one queen bed, TV, nightstand, dresser, and a bathroom with dressing area.

"Let's see if we can't find the jewelry," Aunt Shirley said.

Aunt Shirley went to the nightstand while I rummaged through the dresser drawers.

Nothing.

"You check the bathroom," Aunt Shirley instructed. "I'll look through his suitcase."

I crinkled my nose. "Why do I have to be the one stuck with going through his dentures and old man products?"

"Stop your whining. I'm digging through his underwear. Do you want that job?"

Without another word, I turned on my heel and walked into the bathroom.

"That's what I thought," Aunt Shirley said.

Stepping into Arthur's bathroom was like stepping back in time. His antique shaving kit was resting on the counter, as was his aftershave. A smell that brought back memories of the old men at church. Let's just say it wasn't a *young* spice I was smelling. But it was the powder that nearly had me gagging. I didn't even want to *imagine* on what body part he was putting the powder.

"Found them," Aunt Shirley hissed.

I ran out of the bathroom to where she had been rummaging through his suitcase. Inside a clear baggie were three rings.

My eyes nearly crossed in my head. "Dang! I sure wish we could take these and just stop this ridiculous escapade right here."

"But we can't," Aunt Shirley said. "We need to take him by surprise tonight. We need to make sure we have enough blackmail to threaten him with."

"I know." I lifted the rings and scrutinized them. They were each lovely in their own way. It nearly broke my heart to think I couldn't take them with me and give them to their rightful owners.

Aunt Shirley laid her hand on my shoulder. "Honey, I promise you these ladies will get their jewelry back. Don't you worry."

I blinked back tears. I don't know if it's because I knew I'd be devastated if something happened to the beautiful engagement ring Garrett gave me or what...but there was no denying I was emotionally attached to this assignment.

"I want you in here hiding in the tub," Aunt Shirley said. "This way you can record what's going on and you can take pictures real quick if we need them. Just run around the corner and start snapping that camera phone."

"You got it. I'll be here and do what's necessary. Don't you worry."

***

"Hey, Sin. How's everything going?" Garrett asked.

Relief flooded me at the sound of Garrett's voice. Not because I was scared for him or me...I just felt an overwhelming urge to hear the soothing timbre of his voice next to my ear.

"Humiliatingly."

Garrett chuckled. "What?"

"After brunch Aunt Shirley took me on a horrific ride the hotel has and I threw up everywhere. She called it my marriage metaphor."

"I'm sorry."

"Me, too. Anyway, I'm back at the suite resting up." I looked at the clock on the hotel alarm. It was still early afternoon. "We're going to dinner tonight around six-thirty, and then we're doing our sting around seven tonight."

Garrett sighed. "I'm aware."

I heard a female's voice in the background.

"What's that noise?" I asked suspiciously.

"Nothing for you to worry about," Garrett said.

"Are you at a bar or something, doing a little bachelor party thing?"

Garrett snickered. "Not hardly. Listen, I have to get off here, but I want you to promise me you won't do anything rash tonight when you try and capture this thief."

I crossed my fingers. "Of course! You know me. I'm not going to do anything stupid."

Silence.

"I love you, Ryli Jo."

My heart stuttered. "I love you, too. More than I can say."

"I gotta run."

"I'll be careful," I said. "I promise."

Garrett grunted. "Take care."

***

"Wow," Paige said as I strode out of the bathroom to where she was sitting on her side of the bed. "I love that color on you. You look beautiful."

The last part came out on a wail and sudden flood of tears. I self-consciously swept a hand down the teal, maxi halter dress. "Umm…somehow I don't feel beautiful."

Paige laughed through a hiccupped sob. "I can't help it! It's all the hormones and crap pulsing through my body. I'm jealous you look so freakin' fabulous, but at the same time I'm so awed how beautiful you look." She brushed tears off her cheeks. "I just can't help it. And I feel like a damn whale in this dress."

Paige had on a floral chiffon maternity dress that stopped just short of her knees. It cinched under her bust, enhancing the twins' soon arrival to anyone who looked at her. She looked glowing and gorgeous, but she'd never believe me if I said so.

I glanced at the time on my cell phone. Paige and I were meeting Mom, Mindy, and Aunt Shirley downstairs around six-thirty at Ooh La La. We were going to grab a quick bite and stay until Arthur arrived. Once he arrived, I was making tracks for his hotel room to get in place. Aunt Shirley would make a move as soon as possible and get Tisdale up to his room. From there, Arthur Tisdale was fair game!

I helped Paige off the bed and grabbed my clutch. "Have you talked to Matt this afternoon?"

Paige rolled her eyes and scowled. "For a second. He said it was pretty busy at the station and that he couldn't chat long. Probably a secret bachelor party for Garrett or something. He'll spend tonight with a young, perky, non-pregnant girl dancing around just for Matt."

I busted out laughing at her pitifulness. "I doubt that's happening. But I will say, when I asked Mom if she'd spoken to

Doc, she said the same thing. That Doc couldn't talk long because he had to run. I wonder what they're up to?"

"Well, I can guarantee you it's nothing as ridiculous as what we are about to do. This is your bachelorette party night, Ryli Jo. And instead of tossing back drinks, you're gonna be crouched in a hotel bathtub ready to toss back an old man."

"An old man who is stealing from nice old ladies."

Paige rubbed her stomach and made a beeline for the door. "I know. And they deserve your help. But I have to agree with your Mom. Just once someone else needs to bear the burden. You should be having fun tonight."

I knew I'd be wasting my breath if I told her I *was* gonna be having fun tonight…crouched down in a tub, ready to pounce on a bad guy!

We took the elevator downstairs and met up with Mom, Mindy, and Aunt Shirley outside Ooh La La. I dug through my purse, grabbed my cell phone, and called Garrett.

It went straight to voicemail.

I tapped out a text asking him to call me back when he could. I then put the phone on vibrate. I didn't want him calling when I was hiding in Arthur's bathroom.

"With this line," Aunt Shirley said, "I'm thinking we just grab something quick, like a piece of pie. This way when Arthur comes in, I can just have a table waiting and you guys can slip out before he notices. I promise to make it up to you."

"That's fine," Mom said. "Mindy and I were on a roll at the Blackjack table. Mindy's won a little tonight."

We all congratulated her as the hostess asked us how many were in our party. We followed the young girl to our table. It was a perfect location to see the front of the restaurant, so spotting Arthur would be no problem.

Our server brought waters and the rest of us ordered coffee—except Paige. She ordered a glass of milk.

"I'm having chocolate cake," Paige pouted. "Not pie. If I can't have coffee or booze tonight, I'm getting something sugary."

"That's showing those kids who's boss," I joked.

Paige scowled and crossed her arms over her big belly.

"What time does the naughty show start tonight?" Mindy asked as she wiggled her eyebrows suggestively at me.

Now it was my turn to scowl and roll my eyes. I didn't need to be reminded that Aunt Shirley had planned a night of wild debauchery and sin for me.

"Nine o'clock," Aunt Shirley said. "I figured we'll have just enough time to apprehend Arthur, return the jewelry, ditch Arthur, and then toss back a bottle of champagne before heading over to the forbidden circles and ropes show."

Mindy giggled. "I grabbed a brochure on the show we are seeing tonight." She fanned her hand in front of her face. "It looks pretty steamy!"

The last bachelorette party had Aunt Shirley sticking dollar bills down a cop's pants. Not a stripper cop...a *real* cop! I just prayed this night wouldn't be as bad as that one.

The waitress took our orders and we chatted about the upcoming plan for Arthur. I glanced once more at my cell phone.

No Garrett.

When the waitress returned with our plates of cakes and pies, I shoved the cell phone in my purse and decided not to worry about it for a while. He'd call when he could.

CHAPTER 14

At five till seven, Arthur Tisdale strolled past the windows of Ooh La La and stood in line to get in. He looked all smarmy in a pair of plaid pants, tan shirt, and red blazer.

"We'll get out of your way now," Mom said. "Ryli, please be careful. I'm still not happy with this plan."

I stood up, kissed her on her forehead and promised to be careful. With one last look at Aunt Shirley, I carefully wound my way through the café and out the exit so Arthur wouldn't see me. Mom, Mindy, and Paige were getting up from the table, too, as I rushed to the elevator.

I checked the battery on my cell phone. Seventy-five percent charged. I'd have plenty of battery life to get everything I needed on video and pictures. A little blackmail just in case hotel security got involved.

I pulled Arthur's electronic key card out of my purse and walked briskly to his door. Looking around to make sure no one was coming, I slipped the key in the slot. The light turned green and I pushed the door open, carefully letting it close behind me.

The room was nice and tidy—a recent change from the last time I was in his room. His suitcase was on the bed, all personal items packed. Even his bathroom accessories. I knew from Cheryl that the senior's yearly trip was over tomorrow. Another reason we had to act tonight.

I took a quick peek in his suitcase. The three rings he'd lifted from Cheryl, Mildred, and Eleanor were still in his possession. Feeling pretty confident, I sashayed slowly around the room, taking in everything, waiting for Aunt Shirley and Arthur to arrive.

I had no idea how Aunt Shirley was going to get Arthur up here, but I had a pretty good idea.

And I gave a shudder at the thought.

Old Man Jenkins would have a fit if he knew Aunt Shirley was going to use her feminine wiles to get to a perpetrator. Good thing he wasn't anywhere around. Garrett for that matter. He'd have a coronary, too.

Arthur's aftershave hit me like a brick wall when I opened his bathroom door and stepped inside. I decided to leave the door open, hoping like heck he wouldn't notice. Not only would it allow the smell to dissipate, but I'd be able to hear the conversation a lot better, too.

I yanked the curtain aside and scrunched my nose. There were still water droplets in the tub and stall where he'd recently showered. That brought an image up that burned my retinas.

Heaving a sigh, I snatched a towel off the rack and wiped down the bottom of the tub so the hem of my dress wouldn't get wet. I made the sudden decision not to take any chances with my party dress and gathered the bottom of the maxi up until the bottom of the dress was at my waist. I then tucked the bottom of my dress into my panties…allowing the excess to billowing out around my upper thighs. My maxi dress was now a mini dress.

I placed another towel on the bottom of the tub and gently laid my purse on top of the towel. I didn't figure Arthur was going to need all these towels if he ended up in the hotel's pokey tonight.

Did hotels have holding cells?

I retrieved my cell phone and patiently stood inside the tub, waiting for something to happen. Luckily, I wasn't disappointed. About fifteen minutes later, I heard someone fumbling with the pull-down lever to get inside the room. I steadied my breathing and switched my phone to video.

And then nearly dropped the phone when it started to vibrate. I had a text message. While I was sure it was from Garrett, I knew I couldn't risk answering it because I was supposed to be recording the video. Ignoring the text, I pulled the curtain aside a few inches and listened in.

"I gotta say, Shirley, those are some lovely pieces you're wearing. Is that a half-carat blue sapphire?"

Aunt Shirley had borrowed jewelry from both Mom and Mindy. I figured if Aunt Shirley didn't nab this guy, when Hank found out about Mindy's stolen ring, he'd come gunning for Arthur something fierce.

Aunt Shirley giggled. "You really know your jewelry, Mr. Tisdale."

I could tell by their voices they'd move farther into the hotel room. I cautiously stepped out over the rim of the tub and tiptoed to the bathroom door.

"I used to be in the business. I worked for a jewelry company for almost thirty-five years. Can you take it off for me to see?"

"Sure."

"Oh, yes. It's lovely."

"Tell me, Arthur," Aunt Shirley's voice purred, "is this all you want me to take off for you?"

I screamed—the sound reverberated throughout the bathroom.

My mistake. The screaming was all in my head.

There was no denying it was creepy hearing Aunt Shirley trying to get all jiggy with Arthur Tisdale.

I felt my phone vibrate again and saw I had another text message. Once again I ignored it and stuck my head out of the bathroom door. Aunt Shirley had positioned herself to face the bathroom, while Arthur had his back to me. Unfortunately, that left me with the unpleasant view of Aunt Shirley's shirt halfway unbuttoned. I could see her satin granny bra.

I crept over to the side of the bed and ducked down for coverage, video still recording.

Arthur had his head bent over the ring, totally ignoring Aunt Shirley's overtly sexual advances.

Arthur finally lifted his head from the ring and stared at Aunt Shirley's half-naked form. "You know, I believe I saw you the other night talking with some of the ladies in this senior's trip."

Oh, no...not good!

I felt my phone vibrate again.

"Oh, really?" I heard the elevated pitch in Aunt Shirley's voice, even though she tried to hide it.

"Yes, really." Arthur said.

He suddenly whipped out a revolver from inside his jacket and pointed it at Aunt Shirley. "So let's cut through the BS. I don't know who you or your ditzy niece are, but you obviously know who I am." He brought his hand up and pointed the gun at Aunt Shirley's forehead. "Hand over the rest of your jewelry, and I won't shoot you."

I let out a gasp. I couldn't help it.

Arthur spun around, and I held up my phone like a shield. "Stop right there. I have everything recorded."

I felt my phone vibrate again and practically wept in frustration. It's like Garrett *knew* I was in trouble and he was gonna make sure I knew *he* knew it!

Arthur took a step toward me, and in the blink of an eye, Aunt Shirley literally went all spider monkey on him. She leaped up onto Arthur's back and tried to grab his gun while they spun in a circle.

I ducked down in a crouch, afraid they'd accidentally shoot me. Aunt Shirley has been known to do that.

Arthur's hotel door suddenly swung open, and an open-mouthed hotel manager stood wide-eyed and shocked at the scene before him. I barely had time to register Garrett, Hank, Doc, and Old Man Jenkins...before the hotel manager let out a scream and fainted.

"Get down!" Garrett shouted. "He's got a gun!"

"Holy crap, lady," Arthur yelled at Aunt Shirley from his hunched-over position. "How much do you weigh?"

"That's it," Aunt Shirley screamed. "You're going down!"

From my squat on the floor beside the bed, I saw Garrett and Hank each crawling on their belly toward Arthur. I don't know what possessed me—maybe it was the fact Garrett never gave me credit for anything, or maybe it was the security I felt in seeing him—but I knew this was my time to show him I knew my stuff.

Without another thought, I threw my phone aside and leaped head-first out of my crouched position to wrap my arms around Arthur's legs. With the leg tackle and the weight of a top-heavy Aunt Shirley on his back…Arthur Tisdale went down with a thud.

Right on my back.

The air rushed out of my lungs and I stopped breathing.

A second later I heard him screaming in pain. I'm assuming Aunt Shirley fell on top of him because I felt another indention on my back…and the inability to breathe was still there.

"Secure the gun," I heard Garrett say.

"It's secured," Hank said.

I *felt* more than saw Arthur being yanked off me. I gasped and sucked in huge gulping packets of air while trying to sit up.

"I think the manager is going to be okay." I recognized Doc's voice, but I was still having a hard time comprehending what was happening.

"What're you doing here?" I asked lamely.

"Saving your butt," Garrett growled. "And I do mean that literally…seeing as how you've just flashed everyone within eye shot."

I'd totally forgotten about tucking in my dress! I scrambled to my feet and nonchalantly pulled the dress out of my underwear.

Hank shook his head at me, then offered Garrett a sympathetic smile. "That's your future wife right there."

"Shut up," I snapped at Hank, trying to fluff out the wrinkles from my dress.

"Shirley Andrews," Old Man Jenkins's voice permeated the hotel room. "You have some explaining to do."

109

A Burning Hot Murder

CHAPTER 15

"What in blazes do you think you're doing?" Old Man Jenkins growled as he took in Aunt Shirley's exposed bra.

"I was using my girlie bits to get answers from this loser! But you've gone and ruined that!"

Hank shook his head at Aunt Shirley. "I saw a lot of brutal things during my twenty-plus years as a Marine. But being forced to see you in a bra takes the cake."

"Oh, bite me," Aunt Shirley grumbled as she quickly buttoned up her shirt.

I chuckled and bent over to pick up my cell phone.

"So I'll ask again," I said as I turned off the video recorder. "What are you all doing here, Garrett?"

Garrett stared at me without smiling. "I got the feeling you might be in over your head. So I—"

"So you what? You thought you'd fly to Vegas and rescue me?" I shrieked. "When are you going to learn I'm a grown-ass woman capable of handling myself?"

I heard Aunt Shirley gasp as the other men in the room suddenly found something interesting on the wall to stare at. Even Arthur Tisdale kept his mouth shut.

Nobody said a word for a full ten seconds.

"I'll start treating you like a grown woman capable of handling herself when you start acting like it," Garrett gritted out between clenched teeth.

Tears sprang to my eyes. On one hand, I wanted to rush to him, hug him, and tell him how much I missed him these last few days. But on the other hand, I was tired of him not seeing me like

Aunt Shirley saw me. Like a woman capable of handling herself in difficult situations.

But I doubt I'd ever get him to see me as an equal. To him, the seasoned veteran and career cop, I was a silly girl who constantly got herself in trouble…and only by sheer luck made it out alive.

"C'mon, Aunt Shirley." I grabbed her by her shirt sleeve. "Let the *men* clean up this mess. I still have a bachelorette party to attend."

"Oh, boy," Aunt Shirley muttered. "I see nothing good coming from this."

Garrett reached for my arm as I went to walk around him. "Please stop. Can we just talk for a minute?"

"Talk about what? About the fact you treat me more like a child than your soon-to-be life wife?"

"That's not fair and you know it."

Loud voices in the hall kept me from answering.

"Did you get our rings back?" Cheryl asked as she and the two other ladies barreled their way into the room.

"Sure did," Aunt Shirley preened. "Just like we said we would." She went over and opened Arthur's suitcase. Unzipping a small travel bag, she reached in and plucked out the rings.

"My ring!" Eleanor cried. "Thank you so much."

"I don't know how those rings got into my bag," Arthur said. "I've never seen them before in my life!"

The sudden appearance of the hotel security guys—thanks to the now-awake hotel manager—and Mom, Paige, and Mindy created an even bigger whirlwind. They were just as surprised as I was to see the men.

By the time the hotel security personnel hauled a howling Arthur away, and Cheryl, Eleanor, and Mildred went along to give their side of the story, the naughty taboo show Aunt Shirley bought tickets for was about to start.

The men followed us to the elevator and rode it down to the lobby.

"Where's Matt?" Paige asked.

"He elected to stay behind with Officer Ryan and man the station," Garrett said, his eyes never leaving me.

"The rest of us decided to tag along when Garrett said you girls might be in trouble," Hank said, looking pointedly at me.

"Now, Hank," Mindy cooed. "We were never in danger."

Hank kissed Mindy's head. "I just wanted to make sure my girl was okay."

Mindy wrapped her arms around Hank. "You old softie."

Doc and Mom were canoodling in the elevator corner, while Aunt Shirley and Old Man Jenkins were shooting daggers at each other.

"We need to go to the show," I said, willing the elevator doors to open.

"The four of us guys have a room on the sixth floor," Garrett said. "After the show, why don't we all get together. You can even fill us in with that restaurant murder you've been talking about."

I snorted. I knew he was throwing me a lifeline, but I'd be damned if I was going to take it.

"After the show, Aunt Shirley has something else planned for me," I said. I was pretty sure it was a lie, but I didn't care.

"That's right," Aunt Shirley said. "Our whole night is filled."

I shrugged my shoulders at Garrett, aware I was being obstinate…but I was so hurt I couldn't help it.

"I'm sure we can spare a few minutes to meet up," Mom said sternly. "How long does the show last?"

"An hour and a half," Aunt Shirley said begrudgingly.

Mom looked at her watch as the elevator doors slid open to the main floor. "Let's meet back here around ten-thirty tonight."

***

"You okay?" Paige asked as we took our seats in the huge auditorium.

Tears filled my eyes, but I quickly blinked them back. "I don't know. A part of me is shocked and honored that Garrett took time out of his own life to come down here because he thought I was in trouble. But the other part of me just wants him to see me for who I am. Who I can be." I turned and looked at Paige. "I mean, we are about to be married, and I wonder if he even knows who I really am."

Paige smiled. "Of course he knows who you are."

I sighed and turned back to the stage. "How can he really...when I still wonder who I am."

Paige patted my hand. "Ryli, it's normal to have cold feet before the wedding, but don't lose sight of the fact that Garrett loves you."

I scoffed. "I don't even know anymore."

Okay. A bit dramatic, but I felt I earned it.

Obviously Paige didn't agree because she rolled her eyes at me. "I never told you this, Ryli, but when you were in the hospital recovering from the gunshot wound you received—"

"I didn't get shot," I interrupted. "I got grazed with a bullet."

Paige glared at me. "When you were in the hospital recovering from the gunshot wound you received, and he was so visibly worried about you, yet so mad at you at the same time...I asked him why he loved you so much."

"Oh nice," I replied sarcastically. "Thanks a lot."

"Hush up and listen to me." She paused for effect. "He said the stunt you just pulled said it all. He said you are stubborn and smart, and it was rare to come across someone who—right or wrong—would give all they had to move heaven and earth for another person."

When I started to argue with her, she held up her hand.

"He told me that's why he loves and respects you. And even when you scare him to death, he said he knows you would put the same care into your marriage with him. You would fight to the death to make the relationship work."

Tears filled my eyes. Now I felt even worse for parting on such bad terms. I had no idea he really felt that way about me. That he saw me as being that strong. Garrett was a hard man to read most days. He wasn't overly talkative about his emotions. He was more the silent brooding type who wanted to solve the problems.

"Do you know we all have love languages?" Paige asked as the lights started to dim and a hush fell over the audience.

"What?"

"Love languages. We all have them. I want you and Garrett to read a book when we get back home."

I crinkled my nose. "How is a book on love languages gonna help me?"

Paige grinned. "Trust me on this. You both need to understand your own love language and then what the other person's love language is. Once you have that down, all your insecurities will fade away."

I wasn't so sure, but as the last of the lights went out, and the auditorium was thrust into blackness, I prayed she was right.

***

"Whooowheee!" Aunt Shirley cried as she fanned herself. "That was one hot show!"

"No doubt," Mindy giggled. "I'm kinda glad Hank's here. We can sneak off and—"

I plugged my ears so I wouldn't have to hear the rest of her sentence. I didn't need to know what my boss and my good friend did in their spare time.

Garrett, Hank, Doc, and Old Man Jenkins were standing together when we walked out of the auditorium. They all looked wary and scared.

"Why're you lookin' like that?" Aunt Shirley demanded as she stood in front of Old Man Jenkins.

Old Man Jenkins cleared his throat. "Because we found out what kind of show you were seeing. A little suggestive wouldn't you say? Half-naked people swinging on ropes and circles."

Aunt Shirley scowled. "I've seen you in a Speedo. Besides, it's a bachelorette party. Don't you judge us."

"We aren't," Doc said quickly as he gave Mom a grin. "We're just wondering what kind of mood y'all are gonna come out in."

Mom sidled up to Doc and laced her arms through his. "A good mood. A really, really good mood."

Doc grinned down at Mom and gave her a quick kiss. "Glad to hear it."

"What about you?" Aunt Shirley demanded as she looked at Old Man Jenkins. "You in any better mood? Because if you aren't, I don't want to be around you. No one asked you to fly here."

"Now listen here, woman. I came here because I was worried about you."

"The day I can't take care of myself is the day you need to—"

"Marry you. I'm aware of what I need to do to you," Old Man Jenkins said.

No one said a word.

Watching the two of them go at it was part comical and part hypnotic. Both were stubborn and tenacious. But if I had to bet money, I think I might put my money down on Old Man Jenkins.

And for some reason, that thought made me smile.

"You men need to leave," Aunt Shirley insisted. "This is Ryli's bachelorette party. No men allowed."

I looked at Garrett and gave him a half smiled. "Well, maybe men can be allowed."

Aunt Shirley threw up her hands. "Unless they're stripping, men aren't allowed!"

Garrett scowled at Aunt Shirley. "We're not stripping."

"Then you ain't staying," Aunt Shirley insisted.

"Actually," Paige said. "I'm really tired. I had a great time tonight. The show was wicked and naughty, exactly how a bachelorette party should be—well, a bachelorette party that isn't mine should be."

I laughed. At Paige's bachelorette party, she constantly warned me I better not do anything indecent or raunchy for her.

"The twins are fighting pretty good right now. And my ribs are losing. I think I'm going to go call Matt and then turn in. You understand, don't you, Ryli?"

"Of course I do."

"Why don't Doc and I go up with you," Mom said. "Make sure you get settled in okay. Then we'll come back down and do some gambling with you guys."

"Sounds good," I said.

"What are we gonna do until then?" Aunt Shirley pouted.

I looked at the time on my cell. I knew this was supposed to be my big night, but the wind seemed to have gone out of my sail.

And I was tired.

Tired of fighting with Garrett about my interactions with Aunt Shirley. Tired of having to defend my actions to everyone. Tired of constantly feeling like my life was at a crossroads, and I only had one choice I could make. But mostly I was tired of constantly putting up walls around myself. It was like I was afraid of being myself for fear of being rejected, so I constantly pushed everyone away—Mom, Garrett, and to a degree even Aunt Shirley.

I shrugged. "Our favorite French restaurant is open for another half an hour. I say we go get some desserts and drinks."

Aunt Shirley perked up. "I like it!"

I looked sideways at Garrett. "Maybe feel out how the murder investigation is coming along."

Garrett smiled at me. "I'd like that, too."

A Burning Hot Murder

The six of us headed over to the five-star restaurant. It was hard to believe that only a few days had passed since we first came to the restaurant.

I grabbed Garrett's hand as we strolled toward the restaurant. We passed the row of posters on the wall, and I suddenly realized with a start where I knew Larry Blackbourn's former assistant from. My heart thudded with the prospect that I might be one step closer to solving this case. If only I knew how the clue fit.

Hank held open the door for us as we piled into the front entrance.

"Welcome," the maître d from the first night greeted us. "Right this way, please."

The majority of the restaurant was empty, except for an elderly couple sitting two tables down from where we were. They looked to be engrossed in their meal.

"Will you be eating a meal or just having desserts and drinks?" the maître d asked.

Aunt Shirley grinned. "Desserts and drinks, of course."

"Very good. I believe Maureen is working still. I'll have her bring in the cart of desserts and she'll take your drink order."

Garrett leaned over and whispered in my ear. "And you've come in here every night because of the great food or because there's still an unsolved murder?"

I blinked my eyes rapidly at him...going for an innocent look. It didn't work. "Okay. You got me—it's both."

"That's what I thought," he chuckled seductively in my ear. "So, who's your main suspect?"

"You really want to know?" I whispered back.

He leaned back and slid his thumb across my lower lip. "I really want to know, Sin."

I shivered at his touch.

CHAPTER 16

"Hey, guys," Maureen chirped as she hurried over to our table. "I was wondering if I'd see you tonight. Looks like you added more to your group."

"This is my fiancé, Garrett," I said. "My boss and Mindy's husband, Hank. And this here is Aunt Shirley's main squeeze, Waylon Jenkins."

"It's nice to meet you all. If you're having dinner, you're in luck, Chef Benoit is back tonight."

I gasped. "Really? So he's not been arrested?"

Maureen's face turned pink as she shook her head. "Thankfully no. Detective Dickerson just gave him a strong warning on going with the police nice and quiet when they ask you to."

"How did Chef Keller take the news he was no longer top chef?" Aunt Shirley asked.

Maureen looked over her shoulder before answering. "He's pretending to be okay, but I can tell he's disappointed." Maureen bit her lip. "I just wish the police would solve this crime so we could all get on with our lives."

"Don't worry," I said. "I think this case will be solved in no time."

"I hope you're right," Maureen said. "Now, what can I get you guys?"

We ordered six chocolate eclairs, a couple crème brûlées, the lemon soufflé, and an apple tart. Drinks were numerous...and all alcoholic.

"Is everyone enjoying themselves?"

I looked up and saw Holly Barrows standing at our table. Tonight she had on a knee-length pinstriped skirt with an emerald green short-sleeved blouse. Her hair was once again pulled back into a severe bun and her glasses were so big they kept sliding down her nose.

"Everything is great, Holly," I said. "We had some unexpected guests surprise us, so we thought we'd bring them in tonight and introduce them to our favorite restaurant."

Holly preened. "Thank you. I feel like things are transitioning smoothly, but it's nice to hear from others."

Holly made small talk a few more seconds before she excused herself.

"So, are you going to tell me who you suspect and why?" Garrett said once everyone else around the table started talking again.

"You promise you won't laugh at me or criticize me?"

Garrett leaned back as though I'd slapped him. "Ryli, I'd never laugh at you. I may not always like the fact you dive head-first into danger, but I'd never laugh at you."

My heart raced at his declaration. "Okay. I think I have it narrowed down to one person, but before I tell you who that person is, let me run some things by you. I think the police and detective in charge of the case thinks Chef Benoit is the main suspect because he and Philippe Bernard were seen arguing with each other, and it's common knowledge they were not on friendly terms. Chef Keller is a suspect because he's been itching to step into Chef Benoit's shoes and become the top chef in the kitchen. By killing Philippe and framing Chef Benoit, he achieves his goal."

I paused as Maureen brought over our drinks, then returned a few minutes later with our desserts. We all began sampling the yummy treats.

Once I had enough sweets for a few minutes, I took a sip of my French Kiss before continuing. "The pastry chef, Chef Quinn, has a lot of anger toward Chef Benoit, Maureen, and Philippe. But outside of pure jealousy, I'm not exactly sure what her motive would be for killing Philippe."

I paused. Garrett seemed to be staring intently at my mouth. I swiped my finger across my lips. "Is there something on my mouth? You keep staring."

Garrett grinned. "I was just thinking your French Kiss looks good. Maybe I should have a taste."

"Okay." I passed him the drink.

Ignoring the glass, he leaned over and kissed me softly, lightly brushing his lips across mine. I moaned when he pulled back.

"You're right, Sin. It's really good."

"Could you two please give it a rest," Aunt Shirley snapped. "There are other people at this table that don't want to see that."

Garrett turned to Aunt Shirley, lifted his eyebrow, then leaned over and kissed me again. I couldn't help the grin that spread across my face when I heard Aunt Shirley harumph across the table.

I drew back and continued where I'd left off. "Then there's Holly Barrows, whom you just met. She *was* the assistant manager, but now she's the manager. Her motive would be with Philippe gone, she could be the manager in charge."

"Uh-huh." Garrett handed me my French Kiss. "Take one more drink for me."

I could feel my face turn red. I glanced surreptitiously around the table, but no one was paying us any attention. I took the glass from him and swallowed the lemony goodness.

I ran my tongue over my lips, and Garrett's pupils dilated. I knew that look. I had a sudden urge to get out of the restaurant and go back upstairs...until I remembered that Paige was sleeping on the other half of my bed.

I stifled a groan and continued. "Lastly, there's Maureen. Even though Chef Benoit and Maureen have been seeing each other, everyone says Philippe had been chasing after Maureen pretty hard. This caused Chef Benoit and Philippe to argue a lot in the kitchen in front of the staff. And right before Philippe was found murdered, Maureen told people earlier that night she was leaving her job."

"Why was she leaving?" Garrett asked. "Did she get in a fight with Philippe or Chef Benoit?"

I shook my head and shrugged. "I don't think so. I haven't got a straight answer from Maureen about why she was planning on leaving. When I asked her about the fact she announced she was leaving, she just simply told me she no longer had that plan."

"What is she hiding?" Garrett asked.

"Exactly. What is she hiding?"

"Who found the body?" Garrett asked as he tucked a wayward curl behind my ear.

I grabbed my drink and swallowed. I knew the seduction game he was playing and I needed courage. "Maureen originally. Then when she screamed, the assistant-manager-now-manager, Holly Barrows, came running in the room."

"And how exactly did he die?"

"The femoral artery in his leg was cut with a huge knife. He also had duct tape over his mouth, and his wrists were duct taped to his chair."

Garrett shook his head. "A cut like that, he'd bleed out in a matter of minutes."

I shuddered at the thought. "The one thing I can't quite figure out is how the knife got by everyone. I mean, it was a huge knife, someone should have seen it. And the police never found it as far as I know."

Garrett picked up his drink and took a swallow. His Adam's apple bobbing up and down.

"What did you say the name of your drink was?" I asked.

"Rusty Nail." He held the glass out to me. "You want a taste?"

A Burning Hot Murder

I pursed my lips together. His drink looked like it could put hair on my chest. I decided to throw caution to the wind and took the glass from him. I took a tentative sip…and nearly breathed fire!

Hank let out a barking laugh. "That drink will kill you, Ginger Snap. You better stick to sipping milk or tea."

I half-heartedly stuck out my tongue at him. Which only made him laugh more.

"Have you solved the murder that took place in this restaurant yet?" Hank asked me. "I need a story for the paper."

I rolled my eyes. "You always need a story for the paper. Besides, Aunt Shirley and I gave you one story tonight. We caught Arthur Tisdale. What more do you want?"

"A story where I don't have to read about your underwear being exposed," Hank countered back.

"Can I get you guys another drink?" Maureen asked as she took a couple plates out of our way. "The restaurant is officially closed, and there's only the chefs and another server here. If you don't mind us cleaning up around you, stay and drink a little longer if you like."

I looked down at my near-empty glass, then over at Aunt Shirley. "One more?"

Aunt Shirley grinned. "One more. Then we head out into the casino to play a little."

"So who is it?" Garrett softly asked. "Who do you suspect the murderer to be?"

I opened my mouth to tell him who I thought it was, even though I wasn't sure how they smuggled the knife in, when I heard the little old lady let out a string of sneezes as she walked toward the exit. Out of habit I called out to her. "Bless you."

She turned around to face me. "Thank you, dear." The old lady daintily withdrew a lace handkerchief from her sleeve, dabbed at her nose, then with a flourish of her hand, quickly stuffed the handkerchief back inside her sleeve. With a smile she turned and walked out the front of the restaurant with her husband.

My heart dropped to my stomach as the pieces of the puzzle suddenly fell into place.

"Omigosh! Hank, get out your pen, have I got a story for you! I know who killed Philippe, and I know how they did it. And I even think I know *why,* but I'm sure there's still more to the story."

"Who?" Aunt Shirley and Garrett demanded at the same time.

"Just call your detective friend," I said to Aunt Shirley. "I'll explain everything when he gets here."

Garrett kissed me softly. "Should I say congratulations?"

Feeling sassy, I picked up my French Kiss and tossed it back. "You bet your tight little tush you should."

Garrett grinned. "Now that's just the alcohol talking."

I grinned back. "Guilty as charged, Chief Kimble."

CHAPTER 17

"Why all the celebration?" Holly Barrows asked as she walked past our table carrying the paid tab the old couple had just left.

I was feeling pretty cocky. "Because I just solved this case. I know who killed Philippe."

Holly stopped walking.

Maureen gasped and dropped the glasses she was carrying, causing the shattered glass to echo loudly on the tile floor. "You know who killed Philippe?"

I nodded. "I do."

"Who is it?" Maureen demanded. "Who killed Philippe?"

Holly stepped behind Maureen so quickly I didn't even see it happen. Not until Maureen started screaming did I realize that Holly had snagged a knife off our table.

"You just couldn't leave it alone, could you?" Holly demanded. "You and your aunt had to stick your nose in where it didn't belong."

Daisy barreled through the swinging doors. "Maureen, is everything okay out here? I heard the crash and thought…" Her voice trailed off when she saw the knife pointed at Maureen's throat.

Then Daisy let out a blood-curdling scream.

"Shut up!" Holly hissed, then cursed when Chef Benoit and Chef Keller came running out of the kitchen.

"Get in here," Holly demanded. "Where's Chef Quinn?"

Chef Benoit cleared his throat, his eyes wide with fear. "She has her earbuds in cleaning up her space. She didn't hear anything. Please don't hurt, Maureen."

"You do as I say and I won't," Holly said. "Now, nice and easy, I want you three to take a seat at the table here."

While the chefs and Daisy gathered up chairs, I looked frantically at Garrett.

"Stay calm," he whispered. "I have everything under control."

Holly lifted the sharp knife and pointed it at Garrett. "Shut up, I said! I need to think!"

Garrett lifted his hands in the air, and Holly went back to resting the knife at Maureen's throat.

"Why?" Maureen whispered. "Why kill Philippe? He was a good man."

Holly rolled her eyes. "He was a liar. I heard him that night. The night I killed him. I heard what he said to you, Maureen."

Maureen's eyebrows lowered in concentration. "What do you mean?"

"I overheard you two talking Monday night. He asked if you'd finally made up your mind to go to management school. I knew then I had to nip this in the bud. So I came prepared Wednesday night. I just didn't know if I'd have the strength to go through with it or not. But then I happened to overhear you in his office about an hour before I killed him. He told you he had a place for you."

Maureen's mouth dropped open. "You killed Philippe because he suggested I go to management school?"

Holly spat. "I killed him because he all but promised you a place at the restaurant. *My* place." Her eyes turned dark. "It's just like a man to go back on his promise. First Harry Blackbourn with his hollow promise to let me be his apprentice instead of sleazy assistant, and then with Philippe. Philippe suggested you go back to school and that he had a place for you. And no way was I going back to shaking my butt on stage in a skimpy outfit and doing lame illusions for drunk audiences."

I thought the illusions were pretty cool.

126

"You stupid, self-centered egomaniac." Maureen clenched her fists in rage. "He never promised me *this* restaurant. He knew I was in love with Chef Benoit and that our relationship couldn't be made public. Philippe also knew I needed to grow as more of an equal to Chef Benoit. So he suggested management school with the promise he'd help get me on at *a* restaurant. Not this one! You killed a good man for a stupid reason!"

Holly Barrows said nothing. All the fight having gone out of her at Maureen's declaration.

"We now know the why," Chef Benoit said, his dark eyes never leaving Maureen's face. "Now how did she do it?"

I suddenly realized Maureen had made a public declaration of love for the Chef and he couldn't really do anything about it now. She must have realized it too, because her face turned red and she averted her gaze.

"Well, don't keep us waiting," Chef Benoit said, his voice as hard as nails. "How'd you do it? You said you came prepared, but I never once saw you carrying or knife, or even being around a knife for that matter."

Holly looked around frantically, as if trying to figure out her best escape route. I looked out of the corner of my eye at Aunt Shirley. I could all but see the wheels turning in her pink and purple head.

Holly's eyes came back to rest on me. "How did you know?"

"I recognized you tonight when I walked past the poster out in the casino lobby. And it just sort of clicked with me. Your hair is almost always pulled back in a severe knot, but I did see you one night with it down. And right there, as I walked past the poster, it clicked who you were. Take off the ridiculously large glasses, and you're the woman in Harry Blackbourn's posters. I figured with your background in illusions, it would be easy for you to hide something almost in plain sight. I was getting frustrated tonight until I saw the old woman at a table down from us sneeze. After she sneezed, she pulled a lace handkerchief out of her sleeve, dabbed her nose, then shoved it back inside. I suddenly realized for an expert illusionist, that would be an easy enough place to stash a large knife and no one would be the wiser."

"Well, your brain just got you and everyone in here killed," Holly said. "Proud of yourself now?"

Not really.

But before I could formulate a response, the kitchen door flew open and Chef Quinn came strolling out, unhooking her earbuds. "Where is everyone?"

Chaos erupted.

Holly lifted the knife off Maureen's throat and pointed it at Chef Quinn, screaming for her to stop.

Maureen made a grab for the knife, diverting Holly's attention.

Chef Benoit stood up, yelling for Maureen to stop.

Aunt Shirley grabbed the apple tart off the table and threw it at Holly. It hit her on the side of her face. Plate and dessert both.

Holly momentarily lost her balance, and everything sort of played out in slow motion then.

I grabbed a fistful of crème brûlée in one hand and chocolate mousse in the other and let my arms fly. I hadn't been in a good food fight since elementary school. The food smacked both Maureen and Holly in the face, once again diverting Holly's attention.

Maureen dropped to the floor and crawled under a table. Holly swung around and took a swipe at Maureen with the knife. That's when Garrett made his move. Unfortunately, so did Aunt Shirley.

Garrett shoved his chair back and sprinted full tilt at Holly. At the same time, Aunt Shirley leaped up onto the table, ran across the length, and dove head first at Holly.

Too bad Garrett had already gotten to Holly and had her subdued. Aunt Shirley landed on Garrett, the top of her head hitting his face…and all three went down hard.

I could hear Garrett cursing Aunt Shirley before they even landed on the floor.

Chef Benoit took off after Maureen, making sure she was okay.

I glanced over at Hank and Mindy. They were calmly sitting at the table, drinking their drinks, watching the festivities unfold, not seeming worried at all.

Old Man Jenkins was shaking his head and flicking his false teeth in and out of his mouth.

"Get off me you old hag!" Holly cried as she tried to buck Aunt Shirley off of her.

Garrett, still cursing, stood up and yanked Holly onto her feet. Blood was running down his face, but he didn't even acknowledge it. Nor did he acknowledge the desserts that were dripping off his body.

"What the hell do you think you're doing?" Garrett yelled at Aunt Shirley. "Who is the police officer here? Who is trained to react in these situations?" He kept barreling forward, not given Aunt Shirley a chance to respond. "Did I *not* say I had everything under control?"

Aunt Shirley huffed, smoothed down her dessert-encrusted clothes, and turned on her heels to walk back to her chair. She plopped down next to Old Man Jenkins, crossed her arms, and scowled at Garrett.

Garrett turned to me, his eyes taking on a fiery glow. "Call the detective in charge and tell him we have his murderer."

"Sure," I squeaked as I ran back to where Aunt Shirley's cell was on the table. My hands were shaking as I pulled up the contact information and hit send.

CHAPTER 18

"Unbelievable," Detective Dickerson murmured as he finished taking my statement. He turned to Aunt Shirley. "You taught her well. You must be very proud."

Aunt Shirley beamed. "I am. I keep telling her there's something natural about her ability, but she doesn't believe me."

Detective Dickerson smiled at me, making me feel self-conscious. Especially in front of Garrett. I knew how he felt about my investigation work, and the fact he was now sporting a butterfly bandage and the start of a black eye didn't help matters any.

"Thank you," I said, avoiding Garrett's eye.

Detective Dickerson continued. "I'll tell you, Miss Sinclair, the beauty standing next to you was one of the best I ever had the privilege to work with."

I bit back a laugh as I looked at Aunt Shirley's red face. "I know. You remind me every time I see you."

Detective Dickerson gave Aunt Shirley another puppy-dog look. "I always thought she was amazing."

Aunt Shirley leaned up on her tiptoes and gave Detective Dickerson a peck on his cheek. "Thanks, Dickie. That means a lot to me."

The stalwart detective's face turned pink and he shuffled his feet on the floor. "Well, I better go arrest me a murderer." He turned to Aunt Shirley. "Maybe I can see you later? Before you leave Las Vegas?"

Aunt Shirley smiled. "Don't see why not, Dickie."

Old Man Jenkins cleared his throat and looked pointedly at Aunt Shirley, then at Detective Dickerson. "I can think of a dozen reasons why not."

Aunt Shirley scowled. "I belong to no man. Remember that."

"You said the day you needed my help would be the day you'd marry me. Remember that."

Aunt Shirley's face went pale.

Detective Dickerson hitched up his pants. "Well, I better get to the station and get Ms. Barrows booked. Thanks again for the help."

Detective Dickerson sauntered over to where a red-faced Holly was screaming her innocence to the police officers.

"Yes. Thanks for your help," Maureen said as she and Chef Benoit walked arm in arm toward us. "I can't believe Holly turned out to be the murderer."

I smiled and looked pointedly at their entwined arms. "Looks like you two are going to be fine."

Maureen blushed and flung her arms around me. "Thank you. For everything." She stepped back and added. "Next time you're in Vegas, make sure you stop by!"

I didn't have the heart to tell her I never wanted to step foot in Las Vegas ever again.

"One thing I don't fully understand," I said to Maureen. "Why did you tell people you were quitting Wednesday night?"

Maureen looked at Chef Benoit. He gave an almost imperceptible nod.

"The reason why I told people I was quitting was also the reason why Chef Benoit took a break that night, even though he usually doesn't." She tucked a piece of hair behind her ear, her face taking on a pink hue. "I'm pregnant."

I let out a little cry and hugged her. "Congratulations!"

Maureen smiled shyly. "I also knew if word got out while I was still a server, it might make things difficult for Chef Benoit. I decided to tell him that night." She looked over and smiled lovingly at him. "Chef took it rather well, so I figured that was all the answer I needed to tell Philippe I was quitting and going to management school. That's why I was in his office that night. I wanted to tell him our good news."

"Good for you," Aunt Shirley said.

"Well, thanks again for everything." Maureen slipped her hand back into Chef Benoit's and they strolled out the door together.

"Hey," Garrett said as he clasped my arm when everyone else started walking away. "Detective Dickerson was right. You did good tonight, Ryli. I really mean that."

I have to admit…I stood a little taller at that praise. Here I've been wallowing in self-pity the last few days thinking Garrett didn't understand me at all.

"So you realize now you didn't need to come all this way just to flex your muscles?" I teased.

Garrett snorted. "Don't press your luck."

"Admit it," I sang in a sing-song voice. "You think I'm awesome. You want to be me."

Garrett threw back his head and laughed. "I will admit you are the most infuriatingly smart, quirky, hot mess I've ever had the privilege to love."

I calculated the sentence and decided I liked it!

Standing even taller, I gathered up my clutch and followed everyone out into the main lobby of the casino. Even though it was nearing midnight, the casino was lit up like it was noon.

"There you guys are." Mom and Doc waved to us as they strolled over to where we were all standing. Mom frowned when she saw the food splattered all over Aunt Shirley and the butterfly bandage and black eye Garrett was sporting.

"You missed the excitement," Mindy informed Mom. "Ryli figured out who the murderer was and there was a bit of a standoff. But everything turned out okay."

Mom closed her eyes. "Why am I not surprised?"

"I need a drink," Aunt Shirley announced. "No. I need a lot of drinks."

"Me, too," Garrett mumbled.

Mom, Doc, Mindy, and Hank played craps at the table next to where Old Man Jenkins, Aunt Shirley, Garrett, and I ended up.

"Do you know how to play this?" I asked Garrett.

He shook his head. "Not really my thing. I just want to make sure Jenkins here is steady enough to handle your aunt. He's been a little more possessive than normal tonight."

"I noticed, too."

He leaned over and kissed me. "Not exactly how you planned your bachelorette party, is it?"

I shrugged. "I can think of worse ways to spend it. At least no one ended up in jail."

"Careful, the night's not over yet," Garrett cautioned.

"That's true."

Garrett nuzzled my neck before whispering in my ear. "Maybe we can find a little time to be alone tonight."

"How are you feeling?" I asked.

"Don't worry. A couple stitches and a black eye won't keep me from wanting you."

I snorted. "You're such a man."

"Guilty as charged."

I was about to suggest we leave right then and there, but a loud shout at our table startled me.

"It's Aunt Shirley!" one of the cowboys exclaimed. "We've missed you!"

"We sure have," another older gentleman said. "Dice aren't rolling the same without you around."

I heard a possessive growl emit from Old Man Jenkins.

"Oh, you boys!" Aunt Shirley giggled. "You sure know how to make a woman feel good!"

Garrett glared at me. "Your aunt is going to either get me into a fight before the night is over, or she's going to make me arrest Old Man Jenkins for fighting before the night is over."

I frowned at Aunt Shirley. I've always known her to be a flirt, but even I had to admit tonight she was going overboard. Was she purposely trying to make Old Man Jenkins jealous?

We positioned ourselves so Aunt Shirley was down at the end, away from the guys. I motioned over a waitress and we gave her our orders.

Thirty minutes later, we were all officially tipsy, and Aunt Shirley was raking in the dough.

"I'd love to stay longer," I said. "But I'm really tired. I think Garrett and I are going to call it a night."

Aunt Shirley held out her hand. "Hand it over."

I frowned. "Hand what over?"

"The key to Arthur Tisdale's room." She picked up her second drink in half an hour and knocked the last of it back. "You still have it, don't you?"

"Yes." I dug in my purse and gave her the electronic key card.

"Cheryl texted me a few minutes ago and said hotel security was holding Arthur overnight until everything could get settled." Aunt Shirley looked over at Old Man Jenkins, a twinkle in her eye. "I'm thinking it would be a shame to let that room go to waste since it's paid for."

Old Man Jenkins's eyes never left Aunt Shirley's. "Agreed."

Aunt Shirley motioned the waitress over and gave her another drink order. "So, figured the old man and I can stay there. You go tell your mom she and Mindy can separate rooms so the men can stay with them. That leaves you and Garrett the room the men rented on the sixth floor."

I had to admit, the plan sounded good to me. Maybe my bachelorette party would end with fireworks after all!

The waitress came by with Aunt Shirley's drink. I frowned at how quickly she was knocking them back. "You go easy on those." I turned to Old Man Jenkins. "Don't let her get too crazy."

He stared intently at me. "Sometimes a person has to let their inhibitions down to truly get what they want."

I cocked my head at him, unsure of what he meant by that.

"Go have fun," Aunt Shirley shooed. "I got everything I need…booze, rolling dice, and a decent enough man."

I laughed and kissed Aunt Shirley on the cheek. "You have fun. Thanks for everything. Tonight was a lot of fun. We apprehended a thief, saw a naughty show, and captured a killer."

"Who knows," Old Man Jenkins said, "maybe something even more exciting can happen before the night is over."

The old man has officially lost his mind.

"Sure!" I said, humoring him.

I gave him a kiss on the cheek, then went over to Mom's table.

"We're not doing too good," Mom laughed. "I think I'm down like forty dollars. Doc, too."

I glanced at the pile of chips in front of Hank. "Looks like you're doing okay, Hank."

He grunted at me.

I filled them in on Aunt Shirley's idea. By the time we said goodnight and finally made our way to Garrett's room, I was tired and my buzz had worn off.

"Have I told you lately that I love you?" Garrett asked as he opened the hotel door to let me in.

I grinned and flipped on a lamp. "Nope. In fact, I was beginning to wonder if we should continue this farce and go through with the wedding after all."

He chuckled and threw the electronic key card on the desk. His hands drifted up to his button-down shirt and he slowly started to unbutton. "Well, then let me tell you, Ryli Jo Sinclair, soon to be Kimble, I do. I love you with all my heart."

I didn't wait for him to continue with his shirt. I launched myself into his arms, knocking him over onto the bed with my force. He groaned when I landed on top of him.

"What is it about you women tonight? It's like you're dead set on beating me up."

I grinned down wickedly at him. "How about I make it up to you?"

***

"Ryli, it's morning. We should probably get around and see what everyone wants to do for breakfast."

I heard Garrett's voice rumbling in my ear. And while it did delicious things to certain parts of my body, I really didn't want to leave the comfort of the warm bed.

"Ryli. Don't make me bring out the water."

I popped my eyes open. "You wouldn't dare."

He chuckled and got off the bed. "I might."

He was already dressed in dark jeans and a white button-down shirt. The sleeves were rolled up on his forearms, exposing his strong arms and hands. His short, jet-black hair was still damp and sticking up in tiny spikes, and he hadn't shaved.

He looked amazing.

"I'd kiss you," I said as I flung the cover aside and got out of the bed. "But I'm sure I have morning breath."

Garrett smiled and shook his head. "Go wash up. I'll try and get ahold of everyone and see what's going on."

"What time does your plane leave today?" I still couldn't believe they flew all this way for one night just because they were concerned for our safely.

"Around one. Do you think you can drive us to the airport? We just have carryon bags."

"Yep. The hotel will hold our bags until we are ready to leave, so I'll just drop you guys off then come back and get the girls."

It only took me a few minutes to get ready. I didn't have my toothbrush handy, so I did a little finger brushing, swished around some mouthwash, then called it good.

"What's everyone doing?" I asked when I walked out of the bathroom a few minutes later.

"Your mom and everyone is about ready to grab some breakfast. However, no one can seem to get ahold of Aunt Shirley."

I groaned. "Goodness only knows."

I picked up my phone and sent her a text. When I didn't hear anything, I tried calling. It went straight to voicemail.

I sighed and figured I better go check on her. "I'll go over to Arthur's room and see what's going on."

"You want me to go?"

I rolled my eyes. "I'm sure I can get there without running into trouble."

Garrett lifted a brow…but said nothing else.

I grabbed my dress up off the other bed and quickly put it on. "I'll be back in about fifteen minutes."

"Sounds good."

I took the elevator to Arthur's floor and strolled over to his room number. I was about to knock when Cheryl, Eleanor, and Mildred lumbered down the hall to where I was standing.

"We're so glad we ran into you," Cheryl said as she gave me a hug.

"Were you looking for us, dear?" Eleanor asked.

"Oh." I suddenly realized they had no idea why I'd be on that floor, and I didn't want them to know about Aunt Shirley's rendezvous in Arthur's room. "Yes. I was just seeing how everything worked out."

"It couldn't have been better," Cheryl said. "We finally got everything taken care of. It took us quite a while to convince the hotel security to not press charges, because if the police came, we were afraid they might take our rings for evidence."

My heart quickened at the thought of Arthur maybe coming back to his room after all and Aunt Shirley and Old Man Jenkins being there. Is that why no one could reach them? Had Arthur come back and done something to them?

I tapered down my fear and tried to get rid of the ladies without seeming rude. "Well, I'm glad it all worked out. I'm just sorry he was free to go. I thought Aunt Shirley said he was going to be detained with security."

The ladies grinned wickedly at each other.

"He wasn't exactly free to go," Mildred assured me. "The hotel security kept him overnight in their holding room. Which is really just a broom closet."

The girls all giggled.

"So Arthur wasn't released to come back to his room?" I asked.

"Nope," Cheryl said. "He's probably still sitting in that closet."

Hope surged through me. There must be another reason why Aunt Shirley wasn't answering her cell phone. Anxious now more than ever, I turned to act like I was going back to the elevator.

"We were just heading downstairs to breakfast," Cheryl said. "Do you and your aunt want to eat with us?"

I racked my brain with an appropriate response to get out of the situation without raising any red flags.

"No thanks. We are going to head back to Missouri later today, so I need to get back upstairs to my suite and pack."

I followed them to the elevator and pushed the up arrow as they pushed the down arrow. Luckily the down elevator came first. I waved as they got on the elevator. Once the doors closed I took off like my hind end was on fire back down the hall to Arthur's room.

Bam! Bam! Bam!

My heart raced as I waited for Aunt Shirley to open the door. I was about to pound again when the door swung open.

"What the hell do you want?" Aunt Shirley growled. "It's still dark out."

I took in her appearance and shuddered. Her purple and pink hair was sticking out in spikes, and if I wasn't mistaken, she had nothing on under the robe she was wearing. I knew this because I could see things I shouldn't ever have to see peeking out from the loosely belted knot.

"Where did you get that robe?" I asked.

Aunt Shirley shrugged. "I guess it's Arthur's. I found it when I got up to see who the heck was pounding on the door at an ungodly hour."

She waved me inside. Old Man Jenkins was still sleeping. At least I assumed he was sleeping. When you get to be that old, I guess it becomes a toss up between sleeping or death.

"We're all ready to eat breakfast," I said. "We couldn't reach you on your cell phone."

Aunt Shirley shrugged. "I guess it's dead. I don't have a charger." She looked over at Old Man Jenkins' prone, still form lying silently in the bed. "I hope that's not a foreshadowing of, like, this old geezer being dead, too."

I giggled. Nervous laughter. I sometimes couldn't help it. "I can't believe you finally hooked up with Old Man Jenkins."

Aunt Shirley shuddered. "Me, either. It must have been a lot crazier night than I even remember." Aunt Shirley furrowed her brow. "In fact, I don't really remember much of anything from last night."

I frowned at her confused look. "You don't? Well, when I left you at the craps table you were winning and drinking like there was no tomorrow."

Aunt Shirley shrugged again, her robe opening up even more. I rubbed my eyes in defense and thought of bunnies running in a field to clear my eyes and give me happy thoughts.

Aunt Shirley cackled. "I guess it's a good thing they say what happens in Vegas stays in Vegas."

Aunt Shirley swiped her hands through her multi-colored spikes.

My gaze fell to her hands, and I let out a little scream. I pointed down at her hands. "Omigod! What *is* that!"

"What?" Aunt Shirley looked down at her robe then patted herself down. "I don't see or feel anything."

"Your hand!" I screamed.

Aunt Shirley brought her hand up and screamed right along with me.

Old Man Jenkins sat up in bed and grinned. "Morning, wifey!"

CHAPTER 19

"Married?" Mom asked for a third time. "You're sure?"

I nodded. "I'm sure."

Once I'd gotten Aunt Shirley calmed down enough she wasn't going to kill Old Man Jenkins, I told them we'd all meet at Ooh La La Café in half an hour. I then hightailed it straight to Momma. I texted Garrett and told him he was needed immediately at the suite.

Once Garrett arrived, I filled everyone in on what I knew so far...and it wasn't much.

"We're gonna have to wait until breakfast to find out everything," I said. "But I'm telling you. I saw the ring, she saw the ring, and Old Man Jenkins called her wifey! Aunt Shirley is married!"

"I just can't get over this," Paige said, trying to hold back her laughter.

"Me, either," Mindy agreed. "What the heck happened after we left them last night?"

"That's right," I said. "You guys were all still playing. What time did you last see them?"

Mom looked at Doc.

Doc shrugged. "Maybe one-thirty. That sound right to you, Hank?"

Hank grinned and shrugged. "I guess so. Talk about a SNAFU. This takes the cake."

"Married," Paige said, shaking her head and rubbing her stomach.

Hank slapped his hand down on the table. "Maybe she'll want to honeymoon with you and Garrett!"

"You shut your mouth right now Hank Perkins!" I cried. "Don't you *even* make that suggestion!"

Garrett let out a low growl and glared at Hank. Unfortunately, Hank didn't seem to care and continued grinning like an idiot.

Mindy looked at her watch. "We should head on down. I definitely don't want to keep them waiting. I need to hear this story."

"Speaking of stories," I said to Hank. "You basically have three. Aunt Shirley and I catch a thief, Aunt Shirley and I capture a killer, and now Aunt Shirley gets married. This should keep you happy for a while."

"What would make me happy would be a foursome honeymoon," Hank laughed and slapped the table again.

It took us less than three minutes to hop on the elevator and practically sprint to the café. Aunt Shirley and Old Man Jenkins were standing in front of the restaurant, both trying to yank open the door, and arguing loudly.

"Well now, this looks like a nice start to wedded bliss," Garrett said sarcastically.

Aunt Shirley turned to glare at Garrett. "I'm trying to tell this overgrown baboon that I don't need no man to hold the door open for me. I can hold my own door open."

Old Man Jenkins lifted a brow but said nothing.

Aunt Shirley scowled again. "Well, I can!"

"And now that you're my wife—"

A collective gasp went up. We now had actual confirmation of the marriage.

"Fine!" Aunt Shirley yanked her hands off the door and crossed them over her sagging chest.

"Nice ring," Paige said.

Aunt Shirley uncrossed her arms and put them behind her back.

I chuckled at her antics. But Old Man Jenkins took it in stride and held the door open for us all.

We found seating at a large table and gave our drink orders to the server.

Garrett looked over at Mom. "I've asked Ryli if she can drop us off at the airport around noon, since we fly out a little after one. Is that okay with you, Janine?"

"Of course," Mom said. "Or I can take you guys. It's no biggie either way."

The waitress came over and plunked coffee mugs down in front of us, then began pouring coffees all around.

"So did you wear a traditional white dress for your wedding?" Hank teased Aunt Shirley.

Aunt Shirley glared at Hank. "Can it, Perkins. I don't want to talk about the dubious surroundings of my tragic death."

I choked on my coffee. "A little dramatic, don't you think?"

Aunt Shirley turned to stare at Old Man Jenkins. "Nope."

He just grinned.

By the time our order was taken and the food arrived, I could tell Aunt Shirley was ready to explode. While she usually loved being the center of attention, she definitely wasn't settling into married life very well.

The boys left to pack their bags while the girls headed back to the suite. We also had to be checked out by eleven-thirty, and there was still a lot of last-minute items to get around.

"I can't believe in two weeks you'll be Ryli Kimble," Paige sighed dramatically as she plopped down on the couch.

Everyone was packed, the bellhops had come to take our bags down to the holding room, and we had a few minutes to spare before meeting up with the guys.

I smiled. "I know. I'm scared but excited."

"Let's just hope everything goes off without a hitch," Mom said. "Sometimes your life is about as smooth as chunky peanut butter."

We all laughed, but I couldn't help but think she was right. I prayed nothing cataclysmic would happen in the days leading up to my big day with Garrett.

I said my goodbyes to the beautiful suite that had been my home for the last few days, then followed the girls to the elevator and out into the lobby of the casino.

"Are you boys ready?" Mom asked. "I think I'm going to take you and let the girls stay here and gamble one last time."

"You have enough money, dear?" Old Man Jenkins teased Aunt Shirley. "Or do you need a little play money?"

Aunt Shirley's face turned purple. She pulled out a voucher, turned to the nearest slot machine, and slid the voucher in. Without saying a word, she pushed the button and the machine started spinning.

"The day I need your money is the day you can take me out back and—"

Aunt Shirley didn't get a chance to finish her sentence. All of a sudden lights and sirens started screaming and blaring from her machine. She looked down at the machine then staggered, clutching her heart.

"I just won five thousand dollars!"

Paige and I started screaming and jumping up and down along with Aunt Shirley. Well, I did most of the jumping, Paige just screamed.

"I won five thousand dollars!" Aunt Shirley sang out in a sing-song voice as she did a jig in front of the machine. "I won five thousand dollars!" She did a twirl and gyrated her hips before turning back to face the machine.

Old Man Jenkins walked up behind her and gave her a little pat on the butt. "Technically, wifey, you only won twenty-five hundred. Half of that is mine now that we're married."

My mouth dropped open as Garrett and Hank busted out laughing. Doc hid his smile in Mom's hair.

"Why you arrogant, no good, son-of-a-toad, lily-livered, little—"

Old Man Jenkins leaned down and gave Aunt Shirley a quick kiss on the cheek. "See ya at home, darling."

The men walked away, Hank and Garrett still laughing, and Doc shaking his head. I turned to Aunt Shirley, who still sputtered with shock and anger.

"Well," I said, "your life definitely won't be dull anymore."

ABOUT THE AUTHOR

Jenna writes in the genre of cozy/women's literature. Her humorous characters and stories revolve around over-the-top family members, creative murders, and there's always a positive element of the military in her stories. Jenna currently lives in Missouri with her fiancé, step-daughter, Nova Scotia duck tolling retriever dog, Brownie, and her tuxedo-cat, Whiskey. She is a former court reporter turned educator turned full-time writer. She has a Master's degree in Special Education, and an Education Specialist degree in Curriculum and Instruction. She also spent twelve years in full-time ministry.

When she's not writing, Jenna likes to attend beer and wine tastings, go antiquing, visit craft festivals, and spend time with her family and friends. You can friend request her on Facebook under Jenna St. James, and she has a blog http://jennastjames.blogspot.com/. You can also e-mail her at authorjennastjames@gmail.com.

Jenna writes both the Ryli Sinclair Mystery and the Sullivan Sisters Mystery. You can purchase these books at http://amazon.com/author/jennastjames. Thank you for taking the time to read Jenna St. James' books. If you enjoy her books, please leave a review on Amazon, Goodreads, or any other social media outlet.

Made in the USA
Columbia, SC
25 August 2018